# THE BOBBSEY TWINS'
## MYSTERY ON THE DEEP BLUE SEA

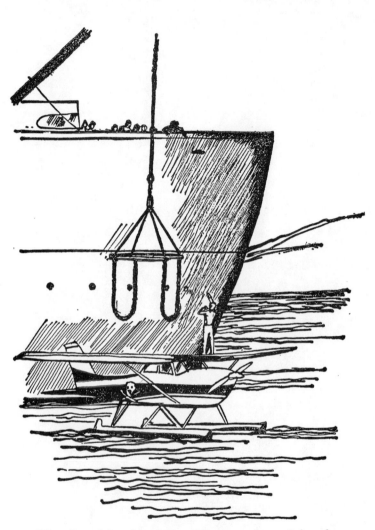

The pilot of the plane had crawled up on one of the wings

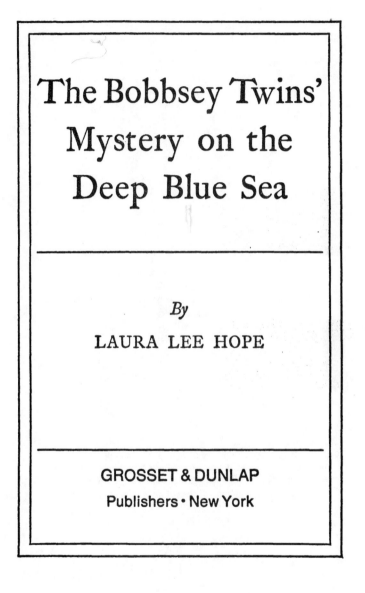

# The Bobbsey Twins' Mystery on the Deep Blue Sea

*By*

LAURA LEE HOPE

GROSSET & DUNLAP
Publishers • New York

Published in 2004 by Grosset & Dunlap, a division of Penguin Young
Readers Group, 345 Hudson Street, New York, New York 10014.
GROSSET & DUNLAP is a trademark of Penguin Group (USA) Inc.
THE BOBBSEY TWINS® is a registered trademark of
Simon & Schuster, Inc.

Printed in the U.S.A.

ISBN 0-448-43762-7

3 5 7 9 10 8 6 4 2

# CONTENTS

# CHAPTER I

## AN ISLAND MYSTERY

"BERT!" Nan Bobbsey called as her twin came whistling up the front walk of their home in Lakeport. "You have a letter from the West Indies—from Kingston, Jamaica!" She waved a white envelope.

"I have?" Bert broke into a run, his dark eyes shining with excitement. "Let's see it!" He took the envelope from his sister's hand and eagerly tore it open.

Bert and Nan were twelve years old, dark and slender. The other pair of Bobbsey twins were six-year-old Freddie and Flossie. They had blond, curly hair and blue eyes.

"Is it from Phil? What does it say?" Nan could not wait for Bert to finish reading.

"Yes, it's from Phil," Bert replied, "and he has sent his picture." Bert passed his sister a photograph as he continued to pore over the letter.

Then he looked up excitedly. "Phil has a pirate mystery!"

"He's very good-looking," Nan said, gazing dreamily at the snapshot. Then she realized what Bert had said. "What is the mystery?" she asked quickly.

Bert and Nan's class in school had been studying about the West Indies. At the suggestion of their teacher, Miss Vandermeer, some of the class had adopted "pen pals" in the various islands. Bert's pal was a fourteen-year-old boy named Phil Henderson, who lived in Kingston.

"Come in the house," Bert suggested, "and I'll read you the letter. I think the other members of the Bobbsey Detective Club should hear it too."

"Okay," said Nan. "Freddie and Flossie are in the kitchen talking to Dinah."

Dinah Johnson was the jolly woman who helped Mrs. Bobbsey with the housework. She was always interested in the twins' adventures. Dinah's husband Sam worked for Mr. Bobbsey in his lumberyard, which was located on the shore of Lake Metoka.

When Bert and Nan walked into the large kitchen Dinah was mixing batter for cookies. Freddie and Flossie were watching hungrily.

"Bert has a letter from Phil Henderson in Jamaica," Nan announced. "He thought you'd like to hear it."

"Oh, yes!" Flossie exclaimed, settling herself more firmly on a stool by the kitchen table. "Read it, Bert!"

Phil had written that he had a sister named Jennifer. She was twelve. Their father had opened a sailing school for children on Henderson Island, just off the southern coast of Jamaica near Kingston.

"Listen to this," said Bert. "It's the most exciting part." He read:

"I have run into a mystery here. It is about pirates and I will tell you more in other letters." Bert stopped.

"Go on!" Freddie urged.

Bert grinned. "That's all. We'll have to wait for the next letter."

"That's mean!" Nan groaned. "What do you suppose the mystery is?"

The Bobbsey twins loved to solve mysteries. During a camping trip *On Blueberry Island* they had found a robbers' hideout. Now they wondered how they could find a solution to a mystery in far-off Jamaica.

"I have a mystery too," Dinah said with a chuckle.

"What is it?" Flossie asked eagerly. "We'll help you."

"My mystery is how am I goin' to roll out these cookies when you're all leanin' on the table?"

The children jumped up. "We'll get out of your way, Dinah," Nan said, laughing.

"Yes," Freddie agreed. "I'm awful hungry for a cookie that's cooked!" He ran from the kitchen, and the others followed.

In the living room Flossie busied herself dressing her favorite doll, while Bert and Nan got out their books and began to study their homework. A few minutes later there was a loud crash from the hall, followed by a groan.

"Freddie!" Nan cried and ran into the hall.

At the foot of the stairs lay Freddie. He was dressed in a pirate's costume.

"What in the world are you doing?" Bert asked in surprise as he and Flossie joined Nan.

Freddie sat up and rubbed his back. "I was being a pirate and sliding down the yardarm," he explained ruefully, looking at the banister. "But I fell off!"

"Are you hurt?" Nan asked anxiously.

Freddie shook his head. "This is my pirate's suit from last Hallowe'en," he said, "so I thought I'd play I was one of Phil's pirates."

Flossie giggled. "You aren't much if you can't slide down a banister without falling!"

Freddie made a face at her and went into the kitchen to see if any cookies were ready. The others went back to the living room. The rest of the day passed uneventfully.

The next morning, at school, Bert met his best friend, Charlie Mason, as he was going in the door. The two boys stopped to talk. Bert told Charlie about the letter from Phil Henderson and the pirate mystery.

"Say, that's neat!" Charlie said. "I wish *my* pen pal was exciting. All he writes about is playing cricket, and I don't know anything about it."

"Phil's interesting, all right," Bert agreed. "I just wish I could go to Jamaica and meet him. Maybe I could help him with the mystery."

A boy about Bert's age but heavier had come up behind them and stood listening to the conversation. Now he pushed past the two boys.

"There's no use your going to Jamaica, Bert Bobbsey," the newcomer said with an unpleasant look. "You can't solve any mysteries!"

"Is that so?" Bert replied hotly. "A lot you know about it, Danny Rugg!"

Danny was in the same class as Bert and Nan. He was not very well liked because he was always playing mean tricks on the other children. He seemed to take particular delight in teasing the Bobbseys. With a rude laugh, Danny went on into the classroom.

When school was over that afternoon, the boys of the two top grades gathered for a baseball game. Sides were chosen. Bert and Danny were on opposing teams.

"Come on," said Charlie, who was captain of Bert's team. "You're pitching, Bert. Let's make it a no-hitter!"

Bert grinned and took his place on the pitcher's mound. Things went well and by the end of the ninth inning when Danny came to bat there had still not been a hit against Bert. His side had three runs!

"This is where your record gets ruined!" Danny jeered, waggling his bat and hunching up his shoulders.

Bert pitched. Danny gave a mighty swing and the ball dribbled off the edge of his bat. Foul ball. "Strike one!" called the boy who was umpire.

Danny glared at him and hitched up his slacks. "Come on! Let's have it!" he called to Bert.

The next pitch was a curve. Danny swung and missed. "Strike two!"

Bert caught a signal from the catcher and sent a hard one right over the plate. Danny jumped back. "Strike three!" yelled the umpire. "Charlie Mason's team wins a no-hitter!"

"No fair!" Danny protested loudly. "Bert Bobbsey tried to hit me with that last pitch!"

The other boys laughed and ran off the field, slapping Bert on the back. Danny, who had the reputation of being a poor loser, sulked and kicked his bat in the dust.

As Bert and Charlie walked home, Danny passed them on his bicycle. "I'll get even with you!" he called.

"If you can't be a good sport, you shouldn't play!" Charlie retorted.

The next day at school nothing was said about the ball game and Danny seemed to be in a good mood. Bert decided that the bully had forgotten his grudge.

That afternoon Bert and Nan walked home together. As they neared the house, Flossie ran out the front door, her yellow hair blowing in the breeze. She waved an envelope in her hand.

"Another letter from Jaca!" she called. "Hurry! Open it!"

Nan laughed. "I guess she means Jamaica. I hope there's more about the pirate mystery in it."

"I haven't answered Phil's last letter yet," Bert said in surprise. "Maybe something exciting has happened down there and he wanted to tell me right away."

Bert slit the envelope and drew out a sheet of paper. Then he gave a gasp of astonishment.

"What is it, Bert? Let me see." Flossie jumped up and down on one foot.

Bert held the paper out so both girls could read the message, printed in large letters:

STAY AWAY FROM JAMAICA.

"What's that?" Flossie wanted to know.

The note was signed at the bottom with a crude drawing of a skull and crossbones.

"What's that?" Flossie wanted to know.

"It's the sign the old pirates used to put on their flags," Bert explained.

"But why would Phil tell you to stay away from Jamaica?" Nan asked, puzzled. "We weren't even planning to go there! And why would he sign a letter that way?"

"I don't think Phil wrote the letter," Bert replied slowly, "but I can't imagine who did. I don't know anyone else in Jamaica and there certainly aren't any pirates nowadays!"

"Let me see the envelope," Nan said as they walked on toward the house.

Bert handed it to her. She studied the address, also printed, and then examined the stamp. "I don't think it came from Jamaica at all," she said finally. "Look, the stamp is cancelled, but there are no marks on the envelope. I think the stamp was taken off another letter and pasted on this one."

Bert took the envelope. "You're right, Nan!" he cried. "It's a trick and I'll bet I know who pulled it!"

"Danny?" Nan suggested.

"Who else? He thinks he's getting even with me for striking him out yesterday."

"Tell him tomorrow he didn't fool you," Flossie suggested.

"I intend to," Bert said firmly.

The next morning when Bert walked into his classroom Danny was already there. He looked at Bert with a smirk. "How are the pirates to-day?" he asked.

Bert smiled. "When did you put that letter in our mailbox, Danny?" he asked.

The bully walked over to Bert. "What do you mean? I didn't put any letter in your box."

"Oh, no? What about this?" Bert pulled the warning note from his pocket. "I suppose you didn't paste the stamp on this envelope."

Danny turned away. "You're crazy. I don't know what you're talking about!"

He pulled a pencil and paper from his pocket as if about to start to work. But as he did, an open envelope fell to the floor.

A collection of cancelled foreign stamps spilled out!

# CHAPTER II

## DANNY'S DUTCH LETTER

BERT pointed to the stamps on the floor. "You seem to have a big collection of used stamps. How many letters are you planning to write?"

Danny squirmed. "Okay, I wrote the note," he said sullenly. "You and your silly mysteries. I thought I'd give you a real one!"

"Make it harder next time!" Bert teased.

At that moment Miss Vandermeer came into the room. She looked at Bert and Danny. "What are you two arguing about?" she asked.

Bert decided not to say anything about Danny's trick. "We were talking over a letter I received from my pal in Jamaica," he said quickly.

"I'm sure we'd all like to hear it, Bert," the teacher said. "Will you read it to us?"

Bert stood up and took Phil's letter from his pocket. The boys and girls listened attentively as he read it aloud.

"That's a very good letter," Miss Vandermeer remarked when he had finished. "You know, children, the Caribbean Sea was the center of pirate activity during the sixteenth and seventeenth centuries, and some of the pirates were based on the island of Jamaica where Phil lives. The raiders became known as buccaneers from their habit of roasting meat over green-stick frames called *boucans*. There were many Spanish ships carrying gold from Mexico to Spain, and these were often attacked by the pirates."

The class sat spellbound as the teacher went on to tell several stories of lawless days in the old-time West Indies.

"We're all interested in Phil's mystery," Miss Vandermeer concluded. "I hope you'll bring his next letter to class, Bert."

He promised to do so.

At the Bobbsey supper table that evening Bert described Danny's embarrassment at dropping the foreign stamps which had given him away. The other twins giggled.

"I wish we could think of a trick to play on Danny," Nan said.

"Yes, let's!" Freddie piped up.

There was silence at the table as the children thought hard to find a good idea.

Finally the twins' pretty mother broke into their thoughts. She remarked, "Now that you're

studying the West Indies, you'll be interested in
a letter I received today from an old friend who
is living in Curaçao. That island is owned by the
Netherlands."

Bert nodded. "We've been reading about it.
In fact, Danny's pen pal lives there."

Nan looked at her twin. "Bert!" she exclaimed. "That's it! That's what we can do!"

The others stared at her in bewilderment.
Bert shook his head. "I don't get it."

Nan turned to her mother. "You still have the
stamped envelope, haven't you, Mother?" she
asked.

"Yes, dear. Would you like it?"

Nan nodded, and turned to her tall, good-
looking father. "Remember that new dictionary
you brought home the other day, Dad?"

"You mean the one that has phrases in all the
foreign languages?" Mr. Bobbsey said with a
smile.

"I see what you mean, Nan!" Bert cried. "We
can make up a funny letter in Dutch and send it
to Danny!"

When supper was over the children excused
themselves and ran into the living room. Nan
looked along the book shelves and pulled out a
small volume. "Here it is!"

Bert got a pad of paper and a pencil, and they
went to work. Finally he held up the finished

sheet of paper. "This should make Danny curious," he said. "Have you fixed the envelope, Nan?"

"Yes." Nan showed him what she had done. The corner of Mrs. Bobbsey's envelope which contained the postmark and stamp had been carefully pasted onto another envelope. This was addressed to Danny in large printing.

Bert examined the result. "Good job, Nan," he praised her. "I'm sure it'll fool Danny. He never looks at anything very carefully."

"Freddie and I'll put it in the Ruggs' mailbox tomorrow morning," Flossie volunteered.

The following Monday morning in class, Bert and Nan looked eagerly at Danny, but he said nothing of having received a letter. And he did not mention it the day after.

"Do you suppose he didn't find it?" Bert asked Nan on the way home.

"He must have," Nan replied. "Flossie said she put it in the box."

The next morning, after Miss Vandermeer had taken the attendance, she smiled at Bert. "Have you had another letter from Phil Henderson?" she asked.

Bert said he had not heard from his pen pal, so Miss Vandermeer looked around the class. "Has anyone else a letter to read?" she asked.

Danny stumbled to his feet. "I have one," he

announced proudly, "but it's written in Dutch."

"My family is Dutch," the teacher replied. "I can translate it for you."

Danny hurried to the front of the room and gave Miss Vandermeer a sheet of paper. She read aloud in a puzzled tone:

*"Kelner snert: Hete bliksem, haringsla, rookvlees. Bonen met uien."*

She chuckled. "I'm afraid, Danny, that someone is playing a trick on you. These words mean:

"Waiter, green pea soup, mashed potatoes and apples, herring salad, smoked beef, beans with onions."

The boys and girls burst into laughter while Danny's face grew redder and redder. He glared at Bert, who was doubled over with merriment.

"You sent me that letter, Bert Bobbsey!" he cried angrily.

"Sure I did," Bert admitted cheerfully. "You wrote me a fake note. I'm just answering it!"

He told Miss Vandermeer the story and she smiled. "I think, though, it would be a better idea to write real letters," she advised. "Danny, I know your pen pal in Curaçao speaks English. Why don't you write and tell him about our school? And you, Bert, ask Phil to tell you more about his mystery."

Bert agreed at once, but Danny took several seconds before saying he would follow her suggestion. Later that afternoon Danny walked past the Bobbsey house on his way home. None of the twins was in sight, but Freddie's toy fire engine lay on the front lawn.

Freddie Bobbsey had loved fire engines ever since he had been able to walk. His father called him his "little fireman" because Freddie always said he was going to be a fireman when he grew up.

Danny eyed the engine thoughtfully. He knew that it was Freddie's most precious toy. "I'll get even with those smarty Bobbseys!" Danny said to himself.

He looked around carefully. The street was deserted. Danny walked over to the fire engine and picked it up. Then quickly he pulled himself onto the lowest branch of a large oak tree. He made his way up a little higher and carefully placed the toy in the crotch where a branch joined the tree trunk. Then he started down.

In the meantime, Flossie and her friend Susie Larker were playing with their dolls in the back yard. Snap, the family's large white shaggy dog which Mr. Bobbsey had bought from a circus man, was asleep under a bush. Close beside him lay Snoop, the Bobbseys' beautiful black cat.

Suddenly Snap raised his head. Then he got up hastily and trotted around the corner of the house. The next minute Flossie and Susie heard him barking fiercely. They put down their dolls and ran to the front yard.

The sight they saw there made them both burst into giggles. Snap was jumping up against the tree trunk, giving sharp little barks. And, hanging by his hands from the lowest branch, was Danny. He was just out of reach of the animal's mouth.

"Call off your dog, Flossie!" Danny yelled. "He's trying to bite me!"

"Snap, come here!" Flossie cried, clapping her hands. "You're a naughty boy!"

Snap gave a final defiant bark and walked over to the girls. Danny let himself drop to the ground and ran down the walk without another word.

"What do you s'pose Danny was doing in our tree?" Flossie asked.

"I don't know," said Susie airily. "Let's go to our dollies."

That evening just before supper Freddie and Flossie ran outside to gather up their toys. Freddie looked all around for his fire engine.

"I'm sure I left it here in front," he told himself, and called out, "Floss, have you seen my engine?"

His twin came from the back yard and shook her head. Then she looked thoughtful. "Danny Rugg was up in our tree this afternoon," Flossie

"Call off your dog, Flossie!" Danny yelled.

said. "Snap wouldn't let him come down until I made him. Maybe Danny took your engine."

"I'll bet he hid it somewhere," Freddie decided.

The twins walked slowly around the front lawn, peering under bushes and in flower beds, but there was no sign of the toy engine. As Flossie passed under the oak tree she looked up. She saw the red fire truck and called to Freddie.

"I'll tell Bert," she said, running toward the house. "He'll get it for you."

In another minute she was back with her older brother. "Won't that Danny Rugg ever change?" Bert said disgustedly.

As the younger twins watched, Bert jumped up and caught the first branch. He pulled himself onto it and climbed from one limb to another until he reached the engine. Then, carefully tucking it under one arm, he made his way down and handed the toy to Freddie.

"Thanks, Bert," the little boy said. "I'm glad my engine isn't hurt."

At supper that evening, Bert and Nan told the others about Danny and his Dutch letter. Mrs. Bobbsey glanced at her husband, then said, "I had a letter from Phil's mother today."

Bert looked surprised. "You did?" he asked. "Why did Mrs. Henderson write to you?"

"Is it something about the pirate mystery?" Nan asked excitedly.

# CHAPTER III

## THE DEEP BLUE SEA!

THE twins waited eagerly for their mother's reply.

"It's something just as exciting as the mystery, I think," Mrs. Bobbsey remarked, her eyes twinkling.

"Please tell us!" Flossie urged.

"Go ahead, Mary," said Mr. Bobbsey with a grin.

The twins' mother said that Mrs. Henderson had written to invite the Bobbsey family to visit them in Kingston. The announcement brought on excited cries and clapping.

Mrs. Bobbsey continued. "Daddy has to go to the West Coast on business, but he wants the rest of us to accept Mrs. Henderson's invitation."

"How super!" Bert exclaimed.

"Oh, Daddy, can't you come with us?" Flossie pleaded, jumping up from the table and going over to clasp her arms around her father's shoulders.

Mr. Bobbsey patted her hands. "I'm afraid not this time, my little sweet fairy," he said with a smile. This was his pet name for Flossie. "But I want you all to go and solve Phil's pirate mystery!"

"Oh boy!" Freddie burst out. "When will we leave?"

"We're sailing on the *Jamaica Queen* a week from Saturday," Mrs. Bobbsey went on. "School closes on Thursday and we'll leave for New York the next day."

"Goody, goody," sang Flossie. "We're going sailing on the deep blue sea!"

In reply to Bert's and Nan's questions, Mr. Bobbsey explained that the *Jamaica Queen* was a cargo ship which took a limited number of passengers. It stopped at various ports in the West Indies to pick up freight.

"It will give you a nice sea voyage and I believe the ship stops at the island of St. Thomas and then Jamaica. It will take about a week to reach Kingston."

"That sounds heavenly," Nan sighed.

"Terrific!" Bert agreed.

A few days later he received another letter from Phil. Bert opened it quickly. Phil said how glad he was that the Bobbseys were coming.

"And listen to this, Nan!" Bert said. "Phil writes that strange things have been happening on Henderson Island. Sails have been cut and holes made in some of the boats. His father has closed the sailing school he runs until the trouble is cleared up."

"Another mystery!" exclaimed Nan. "This is going to be an exciting visit!"

The following week was a busy one. Mrs. Bobbsey and Nan shopped for thin clothes for all of them, since Mrs. Henderson had warned that it would be very hot in Jamaica.

"Send me a postcard and tell me about the pirate mystery," Miss Vandermeer said to the older twins when they told her good-by.

Mrs. Bobbsey and the children planned to fly to New York on Friday and board the ship Saturday morning. Just before Sam was to drive them to the airport, Freddie came up to his mother carrying his small fishing rod.

"May I take this?" he asked. "I'd like to catch a fish from the deep blue sea."

"I don't think you'll have a chance to fish, dear," she said. "And the rod is too awkward to carry."

Sadly Freddie put it back in his closet. But another idea had come to him. He kept it a secret.

The flight to New York was smooth, and the twins enjoyed spending the night in a big city hotel. When they arrived at the dock the next morning they found it a busy place. Passengers and friends who had come to see them off were milling around the gangplank. Burly men were pushing great mounds of luggage along the pier.

Mrs. Bobbsey went up to the booth to show her tickets. Then she turned to the children. "We can go aboard now. Where's Freddie?"

The little boy was nowhere to be seen. Bert and Nan walked around the big dock area. When they came to the open end overlooking the Hudson River, Nan shivered. "You don't think he came out here and fell into the water?" she asked fearfully.

"No, I don't," said Bert firmly. "You know Freddie. He's probably found something that interested him, and he's forgotten all about us."

When they returned to Mrs. Bobbsey and Flossie, Freddie's twin was in tears. "Freddie's lost," she sobbed. "He's not coming to Jaca!"

"We'll find him," Bert assured her. At that moment he noticed a hole in the floor of the dock not far away. It was marked only by a red iron bar. "Wait a minute," Bert said.

He walked over and peered down the hole. There was a small iron spiral stairway leading down to what appeared to be storage space below. As Bert looked a dock man started up the stairs. Behind him was Freddie.

"Freddie!" Bert cried. "What were you doing down there? We've been looking all over for you."

"Gleeps!" said Freddie. "I saw this little stairway and I wanted to find out where it went. There are millions and millions of packages all over the floor!"

"You're not supposed to go down there, and you've worried Mother," Bert said sternly.

"I'm sorry," Freddie said. "Can we go on the ship now?"

Mrs. Bobbsey was so relieved to see Freddie that she did not scold him, but herded all the twins up the gangplank into their cabins. Mrs. Bobbsey, Nan, and Flossie would share one while the boys were just across the narrow corridor.

"Put your things down, and we'll go up on deck to watch the ship leave the shore," the children's mother directed.

When they reached the railing of the main deck they saw a gay scene. The gangplank had been drawn up. Rolls of colored streamers had been handed to the passengers and to their friends on the pier. The paper ribbons were being tossed out and unrolled in long, curling strings. In a few minutes the ship and the dock were linked by the many-colored streamers.

"Isn't it bee-yoo-ti-ful?" Flossie gasped.

The children got rolls of the bright paper from the stewards and soon were tossing them toward the crowd on the pier. Just when all the streamers were unfurled the ship's whistle gave several deep hoots. Dock men quickly unfastened the ropes which were wound around stanchions on the pier, and slowly the *Jamaica Queen* edged out into the broad river.

"Come on, Flossie!" Freddie urged. "Let's go up on the next deck."

"Don't get lost, children," Mrs. Bobbsey called after them. "Lunch will be served soon."

When the small twins reached the railing of the deck above, Freddie said, "I want to show you something I brought with me."

"What is it?" Flossie asked eagerly.

Freddie reached into his pocket and pulled out a ball of string. "This is my fishing line," he explained. "You see, I've fastened a bent pin on the end for a hook."

"That's nice," Flossie said admiringly, "but I thought Mommy said you wouldn't be doing any fishing."

"She just didn't want me to bring my rod," Freddie explained. "She wouldn't mind this string, and I'll bet I can fish over the rail right on

our ship—like this!" Freddie dropped the end
with the bent pin over the rail and slowly un-
wound the twine.

"Let me hold it, Freddie!" Flossie begged. "I
want to fish!"

"Well—just for a minute," Freddie agreed
and passed the ball of string to her.

Flossie dangled the line. Then she stood and
waited as a fresh breeze from the river ruffled
her blond curls.

"Oh, Freddie, I have a fish!" Flossie cried
suddenly as the string stretched taut.

"Pull it up! Pull it up!" Freddie yelled in excitement.

Carefully Flossie hauled in the string and
wound it around the ball. Finally the end appeared at the rail. Attached to the bent pin was a
piece of bright-colored silk.

"Oh dear," Flossie cried. "It's not a fish after
all!"

"I'll take it back," Freddie offered.

The two children ran to the steps which led to
the deck below. From the top they could see a
woman, and a little girl about their age, just
starting up. The woman looked toward the small
twins.

"Why, that's my scarf!" she called to Freddie.
"I'm glad you found it." She laughed. "The
scarf suddenly left my head!"

"Oh dear!" Flossie cried. "It's not a fish after all!"

By this time the woman and the little girl had reached the deck where Freddie and Flossie stood. Flossie spoke up.

"I was fishing with Freddie's line," she explained, "and I thought I had a fish, but it was your scarf! I'm awf'ly sorry!"

The woman laughed as she tied the scarf around her head. "There's no harm done. I'm lucky you caught it." She motioned to the dark-haired child with her. "I'm Mrs. Smith and this is my daughter Karen." The child smiled shyly.

"We're Freddie and Flossie Bobbsey," Freddie explained. "We're twins and we have a twin brother and sister, too. They're Nan and Bert."

"How nice!" Mrs. Smith said with a smile. "I hope you and Karen will be friends. We're going as far as Kingston, Jamaica."

"We're going to Jaca, too," Flossie informed her.

"Flossie! Freddie!" came a call from a nearby doorway. "Come get ready for lunch."

"All right," they told their mother.

The twins said good-by to their new friends and ran inside. By the time lunch was over the *Jamaica Queen* had reached the open ocean. Reclining chairs were set up on deck, and the passengers began to get acquainted.

Bert, Nan, and the younger twins spent the afternoon exploring the vessel. They tried all the chairs in the lounge, examined the books in the small library and traced the ship's course on the map fastened to the wall just outside the lounge.

Finally they came out onto the stern of the upper deck.

"Good!" Nan exclaimed. "There's a swimming pool!"

Freddie ran over and peered down into the open space. "There isn't any water in it," he said in disappointment. "And it's covered up." He pointed to the wide-meshed green net which was stretched over the empty pool.

"They'll probably fill it tomorrow," Bert said.

He was right. Directly after breakfast the next morning, Freddie and Flossie ran out to the deck. The pool was filled with sparkling water, and mats and chairs had been placed around the edge.

As they stood admiring the scene, Karen Smith came up to them. "I'm going to the top deck to see Ginger," she said. "Would you like to go with me?"

"Sure," Freddie agreed. "Who's Ginger?"

"He's my new puppy. My grandmother gave him to me when Mommy said we had to go home."

"Oh!" said Flossie in surprise. "You live in Jamaica!"

"Yes."

On the way to the top deck Karen explained that she and her mother had been visiting her grandmother in the United States. They were returning home sooner than they had planned.

"My daddy wrote that someone was stealing things from his shop in Kingston. He is very worried and wants Mommy and me to come home."

"We'll be in Jaca. We'll help your daddy catch the bad people," Flossie assured her solemnly.

"Oh, thank you!" Karen said. She ran up to a row of wire cages which stood in a sheltered spot in the center of the deck. "Here's Ginger!"

Inside the cage Freddie and Flossie could see a ginger-colored cocker spaniel. The puppy was jumping up against the wire and whining with excitement.

"The deck steward told Mommy he had unlocked the cage," Karen explained. "I'm going to take Ginger for a walk."

She reached for the catch of the cage and unfastened it. The next second the puppy dashed out and headed for the stairway!

"Catch Ginger!" Karen shrieked.

# CHAPTER IV

## AN OCEAN RESCUE

"I'LL get him!" Freddie raced after the fleeing puppy with Flossie and Karen close behind him.

When they reached the next deck they were just in time to see Ginger dodge through an open doorway. The three children followed. Down the narrow corridor, into the lounge by one door and out by the other and up the stairs again the puppy led them.

Long ears flapping gaily behind him, Ginger ran around the deck. Once he stopped briefly to sniff at a life preserver fastened beneath the railing.

Freddie crept forward and was just about to grab the puppy's collar when Ginger was off again! Down the stairs to the swimming pool deck he dashed, through an open door, and with a flying leap landed in the pool!

"Oh, he'll drown!" Karen cried.

Bert and Nan had put on their bathing suits and were stretched out on mats by the side of the pool. When Ginger jumped into the water he dived directly in front of Bert. The boy sat up with a start as water sprayed over him.

"Save Ginger!" Flossie called desperately.

Bert knew the puppy could swim by instinct, nevertheless he jumped into the pool and grabbed the little dog. Then he swam to the edge and handed the dripping Ginger to Nan.

Karen ran around the side of the pool and took her pet into her arms. "Thank you very much," she said to Bert as the boy pulled himself out of the water. "I don't think Ginger knows how to swim."

Bert grinned. "All dogs can swim, but Ginger probably was pretty frightened by his plunge."

Freddie and Flossie went with Karen to return Ginger to the top deck. The steward was there, giving the animals fresh water. He got a towel, rubbed the cocker dry, then put him back in his cage. "You may take him out twice a day for a run if you like," he told Karen, "but be sure he's on a leash."

Karen promised to be careful the next time. She and the small twins said good-by to Ginger and went to join Bert and Nan at the pool.

Many of the passengers were walking around the deck and the children enjoyed watching them. One man, tall and middle-aged, wore a loud black-and-white striped cap. He finally came to the pool and dropped into a chair.

"That man sits near us in the dining room," Nan whispered to the others. "He doesn't seem to be with anyone. Maybe he's lonely."

She got up and walked over to him and smiled. "Good morning," Nan said pleasantly. He did not answer.

In a moment the man in the striped cap got up from his chair and strode away.

"I guess Mr. Striped Cap wasn't lonely after all!" Bert said teasingly as Nan rejoined the others.

"I think he's horrid!" Flossie said indignantly. "At least he could be polite."

After lunch Bert wandered into the small room which served as the ship's library. Shelves across one end held a collection of books. A steward sat at a desk in front of them.

He looked up as Bert came in. "Hello," he said, "are you looking for something to read?"

"I'd like a special book," Bert replied. "Is there one here on pirates?"

"So you're interested in pirates, are you?" The man smiled and turned to a box of cards on the desk before him. "We have a book about Henry Morgan, the famous buccaneer. I think you'd like it."

"That sounds keen," said Bert eagerly. "May I borrow it?"

The steward turned to the book shelves. "I think it's right here." He ran his hand along the volumes. Then he turned back to the cards. "Now that I think about it, I'm afraid I gave the book out this morning to a Mr. Hansen. He asked for it especially. Says he's an authority on pirates. Maybe he'd let you have it when he finishes."

"What does Mr. Hansen look like?" Bert asked.

"He's a tall man and wears a black-and-white striped cap."

"Oh, oh," Bert said with a grin. "I don't think I'll ask *him!*"

Bert selected a book of baseball stories and went into the lounge to read. Nan was seated on the promenade deck chatting with her mother while Freddie and Flossie were in the children's playroom with Karen.

Finally Freddie pushed aside the game of checkers they were playing. "It's hot in here," he said. "Let's go and play on deck."

The girls agreed, and the three ran outside. The place was almost deserted. Only a few people were lying in chairs or standing up at the far end. The children noticed a man by the rail reading a book.

"What shall we play?" Flossie asked, running over to peer down at the blue water being knifed away from the side of the ship.

There were black clouds on the horizon, and the vessel was beginning to roll. Freddie pretended to stumble. "I can't stand up!" he cried. "Let's play tag. It will be fun to try to run."

"Okay." Flossie tapped her twin on the shoulder and darted away. "You're It!"

Karen giggled and ran after Flossie. Quickly Freddie caught up with the dark-haired little girl and tagged her. "Now you're It!" he said triumphantly. "You can't catch me!"

Freddie raced along the deck with Karen after him. As the little boy came near the man reading at the rail the ship gave a lurch. Freddie skidded full force into the man. The book flew from his hands and fell in the ocean far below!

The man grabbed Freddie angrily. He was Mr. Striped Cap! "Just see what you did, young man!" he cried. "That was a valuable book. You can just march yourself in to the library steward and pay for it! *I* wasn't responsible for losing it!"

"Y-yes, sir. I'm sorry, sir," Freddie stammered. Then he turned and ran back to where his mother and Nan were seated. Breathlessly he told them his story.

"You should have been more careful," Mrs.

The book flew from his hands.

Bobbsey said, "but I'm sure it was an accident. Nan will go with you to explain to the steward. If he wants you to pay for the book, come back and I'll give you the money."

Hand in hand, Freddie and Nan went into the library. The little boy described the incident to the steward. "I'm sorry the book fell into the water," he concluded, "but my mother will pay for it."

The steward laughed. "That's all right, sonny," he said. "I don't think we'll charge you for the book. That pirate, Henry Morgan, was no good. He deserves to land in the sea!"

Nan and Freddie thanked the steward and went out on deck again. This time the rail was lined with passengers peering over the side. There was a murmur of excited comment.

"What happened?" Freddie asked, running over to stand by his mother.

"A seaplane just made a forced landing," she said. "I think we're going to rescue it."

The children looked down. Not far away, bobbing in the waves, was a small seaplane. Painted on the side they could see a skull and crossbones.

"It's a pirate plane!" Freddie exclaimed excitedly.

"I imagine the emblem is just an idea of the pilot's," Mrs. Bobbsey told him with a smile.

The captain of the *Jamaica Queen* was leaning over the railing outside the ship's bridge calling down to the pilot of the plane, who had crawled up on one of the wings. After some discussion, a steel cable was lowered on a boom. The pilot made his way carefully to the tail of the plane and secured the cable to it. Then he walked out on the wing and climbed up a rope ladder which had been lowered over the side of the ship.

The pilot hurried over to the boom operator. Then at a signal from the captain, the plane was slowly raised from the ocean and gently deposited on the cargo deck of the ship.

When it was safely down, a cheer went up from the watching passengers. The pilot shook hands with the boom operator and hurried up to the bridge to confer with the captain.

"Wasn't that 'citing?" Flossie asked as the Bobbseys turned away from the rail. They all agreed.

Just before dinner that evening, Bert and Freddie were on deck waiting for their mother and the girls. The captain and the seaplane pilot walked toward them, deep in conversation. Just as they reached the boys, a ship's officer called the captain away.

The pilot turned toward Bert and Freddie

and smiled. He was a stocky young man with a blond crew cut.

Freddie could not resist asking a question. "Are you a pirate?" he queried, wide-eyed.

The young man laughed. "No," he replied, "but one of my ancestors was. I'm Casey Browne. Way back in the seventeenth century one of my great-great-grandfathers was Henry Browne, the pirate."

"Gleeps!" exclaimed Freddie.

"Is that why you have a skull and crossbones on your plane?" Bert asked.

"Not exactly. I painted it on my ship just for fun!" The pilot explained that he was interested in treasure which could sometimes be salvaged from sunken pirate ships. He told the twins that the water of the Caribbean Sea was so clear that some of the wrecks could be spotted from the air!

"I was coming north from such a search when my engine conked out," he said. "I'm lucky this ship came along. The captain is going to take me as far as St. Thomas."

"Tell us some more about Henry Browne," Freddie begged.

"The story is that Browne had captured a Spanish galleon on its way back to Spain with a lot of treasure. Then the ship disappeared. Some think it was sunk near Ile de la Tortue north of Haiti. I've been searching in that area but haven't found any trace of the galleon."

"It must be keen flying around looking for treasure," Bert said with enthusiasm.

"Bert has a pirate mystery," Freddie spoke up proudly.

"That so?" Casey asked. "Tell me about it."

Bert told their new friend about Phil Henderson and his letters. "We don't really know very much about the mystery," he admitted, "but we Bobbseys like to solve mysteries, so we're going to work on this."

"Good for you!" Casey said. "I get over to Jamaica every once in a while. I'll look you up the next time I come and see how you're getting along."

"That'll be great!" Bert beamed at the thought of introducing Pilot Casey to Phil.

"So long. See you later!" Casey waved and walked away.

Freddie and Bert turned to go inside and find their mother. As they did, the boys saw the man in the striped cap slip around a corner ahead of them.

"Now what was *he* doing?" Bert asked in surprise.

"I think he was listening to us!" Freddie answered.

# CHAPTER V

## BLUEBEARD'S CASTLE

"THAT'S queer," said Bert thoughtfully. "I wonder why Mr. Striped Cap was eavesdropping."

The boys joined their mother and sisters and went into the dining room. Freddie told them about meeting Casey Browne. "He's coming to see us in Kingston!" he added proudly.

"I wish I'd been with you," Flossie said wistfully.

"We don't arrive in St. Thomas until Wednesday," Mrs. Bobbsey told the children. "Perhaps you and Nan can meet Mr. Browne before then."

The next morning Bert and Nan decided to play deck tennis. Freddie, Flossie, and Karen met in the playroom. When Freddie told Karen about Casey, she too wanted to meet the pilot.

"Come on then," Freddie said importantly. "We'll go down to the seaplane. I'll bet he's there."

41

But when the three children arrived on the lower deck where the seaplane was tied up, the pilot was nowhere in sight. He had evidently been working on the engine, though, as a small stepladder leaned against the fuselage.

"Let's look inside," Freddie proposed.

"Do you think we should?" Karen asked uncertainly. "Mr. Browne might not want us to."

"Sure, he won't care," Freddie insisted. He climbed up the ladder to the door and stepped inside the cabin. Flossie and Karen followed.

"I'll be the pilot!" Freddie said. He slipped behind the wheel and pretended to move it.

"Be careful, Freddie!" Flossie cautioned.

Karen sat down next to Freddie and peered around the cabin. Suddenly she gasped. "Look!" She pointed to a little carved wooden monkey which hung by one arm from the roof of the cockpit.

"How cute!" Flossie cried.

"It's just like one my daddy had in his shop," Karen told them. "Do you s'pose Mr. Browne bought it there?"

"We'll ask him," Freddie assured her.

As the children climbed out of the plane, the pilot walked toward them. He stopped when he saw the youngsters, a disturbed look on his face.

"Hi, Mr. Browne!" Freddie called. "We've been looking at your plane. This is my sister

Flossie, and Karen Smith. Karen lives in Jamaica."

"Hi, kids! Just call me Casey. I'm glad to see you, but you mustn't climb into the plane when I'm not here. You might do some damage or get hurt."

"We won't do it again, Casey," Flossie said.

Freddie spoke up. "Where did you get the wooden monkey? Karen's daddy has one like it."

Casey looked embarrassed. "Oh, that," he said offhandedly. "I picked it up—use it for a good luck piece. I like monkeys. See this one?"

He pulled a short chain from the small pocket in the front of his slacks. On the end dangled a peach stone. It had been hollowed out into the figure of a tiny curled-up monkey clutching its tail in its paws. The twins and Karen pressed close to examine the little carving.

While the younger children continued talking to Casey, Bert and Nan were having a close contest in their deck tennis. Suddenly Bert slipped and fell to his knees. As he put his hand down on the deck to steady himself, he exclaimed, "My shoelace is broken. That's what made me fall. I'll have to go to my cabin and change it."

"Okay," Nan agreed. "I'll wait here."

Bert hurried along the narrow corridor until he came to his cabin. Hastily he flung open the door. Then he stopped short in amazement.

The man in the striped cap was busily going through a drawer in Bert's dresser!

His back was toward the door, but the click of the doorknob made the man turn quickly. A look of consternation came over his face. He mumbled that he was in the wrong room, hurried past the boy and disappeared down the corridor.

"Well, for Pete's sake!" Bert said aloud. "What was that all about?" He made a hasty survey of the drawers. Nothing seemed to be missing. What had Mr. Hansen been looking for?

Still puzzled at the man's behavior, Bert changed the laces in his sneakers and went back on deck. As he stepped out the doorway he bumped into Casey Browne.

"Watch it there, boy!" the pilot said, grinning. "You look as if you're walking in your sleep!"

"The queerest thing just happened," Bert remarked. "I still can't figure it out."

He told Casey about finding Mr. Hansen in his cabin rummaging in the dresser. "He said he was in the wrong room," Bert added doubtfully.

"That Hansen's a queer duck!" Casey agreed. "He tells me he's interested in pirates. Tried to talk me into taking him along in my plane to look for sunken ships."

Bert shrugged. "Well, I sure don't know what he wanted in *my* cabin!"

The man in the striped cap was busily going through Bert's
drawer.

When Mrs. Bobbsey heard of the incident she was disturbed. "As long as nothing is missing, I don't think I'll report it. Mr. Hansen may have blundered into the wrong cabin, as he said."

The children kept a sharp lookout for Striped Cap but did not see him the rest of that day or the next.

Shortly after noon on Wednesday the *Jamaica Queen* sailed into the harbor of St. Thomas. Mrs. Bobbsey and the twins stood at the rail as the ship docked. Back from the main street the houses of the town of Charlotte Amalie straggled up the steep hills.

Near the ship, the Bobbseys could see a number of waiting cars. The drivers looked up expectantly, hoping for sightseeing customers.

"What would you like to do?" Mrs. Bobbsey asked the children.

"May we see Bluebeard's Castle?" Nan asked. "I've read about it."

"Isn't he the one who is supposed to have killed all his wives?" Bert inquired with a grin.

"I don't think that man ever lived here," said Mrs. Bobbsey, "but I'm told it's a lovely drive up to the castle. We'll take one of those cars."

"I have to get my pocketbook," Flossie said importantly. "I might want to buy something."

Mrs. Bobbsey smiled. "Run along, dear. We'll wait for you."

Flossie dashed off while the others sat down in deck chairs to watch the comings and goings on the waterfront.

"There's Striped Cap!" Bert said suddenly. "See, he's talking to that driver."

Again the boy wondered about the unfriendly passenger—and his odd actions.

Some time passed, then Mrs. Bobbsey said uneasily, "Flossie should be back by now."

"I'll go look for her, Mother," Nan offered and went down to the cabin.

When she reached it the door was closed, but she could hear someone pounding on the other side.

"Flossie!" Nan called. "Is that you?"

"Oh, Nan," came a tearful voice, "I'm glad you came. I can't open the door!"

"Did you turn the lock, Flossie?" her sister asked. "If you did, just turn it back."

"It won't move!" the little girl wailed.

"I'll get someone to let you out," Nan said.

She ran to the end of the corridor. Their room steward was just coming from one of the cabins. "What's the matter, miss?" he asked, seeing her distressed look.

"Oh, Albert!" Nan cried. "Flossie's locked in our cabin and she can't get out!"

The steward took a bunch of keys from the pocket of his white jacket. He followed Nan back down the corridor and opened the door.

"Thank you!" the girls exclaimed.

The steward smiled, waved and went back to his work. Nan and Flossie ran to the deck where the others were waiting.

"We had decided you'd both fallen over-board," Bert said teasingly. "You missed saying good-by to Casey. He and his plane are gone."

"I couldn't open the door and Nan had to get Albert to let me out," Flossie explained.

When Mrs. Bobbsey and the twins reached the dock there was only one car standing there. Mr. Hansen was still talking to the driver. As the Bobbseys came toward him he hurried away.

"Are you free?" Mrs. Bobbsey asked the cab driver.

"Yes," the driver said with a smile. "I take you anywhere you like to go. Charlotte Amalie is a very beautiful city."

"We were delayed leaving the ship and haven't too much time," Mrs. Bobbsey replied, "but the children would like to see Bluebeard's Castle."

The man opened the car doors. They started off, with Mrs. Bobbsey, Bert and Nan in the back. The younger twins were seated in front.

"This *is* lovely," Nan remarked as the car made its way up the steep streets lined with flowering hedges. Houses painted in pastel shades of blue, yellow, and pink could be glimpsed behind them.

After a few minutes the houses became farther apart and a short while later the Bobbseys' car drove through a white gateway and stopped before a modern building. It had been erected around an old stone tower.

"This is Bluebeard's Castle," the driver announced as he opened the doors.

"Looks spooky," Flossie declared.

"I want to climb up in it," Freddie said, running toward the building. The others followed. When he reached the door, the little boy stopped. "It isn't spooky at all," he wailed. "It's a shop!"

The other children were disappointed too when they saw the gift shop. Upon questioning the clerk, Bert learned that the upper part of the tower contained hotel guest rooms.

"I guess there's no point in going up," he said, turning away.

Nan snapped a few pictures of the gloomy-looking building. Then they all went into the hotel restaurant. The Bobbseys sat down at a table overlooking the bay and ordered ice cream.

"*Mmm,*" said Flossie, finishing her last spoonful. "That was yummy."

Suddenly Mrs. Bobbsey looked at her watch. "Gracious!" she cried. "It's almost four-thirty and the ship sails at five. We'll have to hurry."

She paid the bill and they ran out to the car. When Mrs. Bobbsey explained to the driver that they must be back at the dock before five he held up his hand with a smile.

"Don't worry," he said. "I will take you down by a back road. It will be much quicker."

They all piled in and the car started off. After going a short distance the driver turned onto a narrow dirt road. He bumped along this for a while then suddenly the car gave a loud backfire and stopped.

The driver got out and raised the hood. "What is it?" Mrs. Bobbsey asked anxiously.

The man walked back to the trunk of the car and took out some tools. "Just a little adjustment needed," he said airily. "It will not take long."

While the man tinkered with the car the children hopped out and walked up the road, hoping another car might come along to give them a lift. But no automobile appeared.

Finally after almost half an hour the driver slammed down the hood. "Now she goes," he announced cheerfully.

The children got back in the car and it sped down the rough road. In a few minutes they emerged onto the waterfront. The Bobbseys stared in horror.

The *Jamaica Queen* was gone!

# CHAPTER VI

## PHIL'S SECRET

THE Bobbseys looked at one another in dismay when they realized that their ship had left.

"What will we do, Mommy?" Flossie wailed.

"I'll find out." Mrs. Bobbsey paid the waiting driver, then hurried over to a passing policeman. After he had heard her story he ran into a nearby building. In a few minutes he was back.

"The shipping line office has radioed the *Jamaica Queen,*" he said. "She will come back."

"Oh, that's wonderful!" Mrs. Bobbsey cried in relief. "Thank you *very much.*"

The officer smiled. "Perhaps you would like to wait in the park." He pointed to a strip of green across the street. The stranded travelers strolled around, but kept glancing at the water.

"I—I hope the captain doesn't change his mind," said Nan. Only half an hour had passed when she cried out, "The ship's coming around that point of land!"

The family dashed across to watch the *Jamaica Queen* slowly make her way through the channel into the harbor.

As the ship drew near the dock, Freddie exclaimed, "Look at all the people!"

The rail was lined with passengers and crew! When the Bobbseys ran to the end of the pier and waved, a great cheer went up from the watchers.

As soon as the vessel had been made fast, the gangplank was put down. The twins and their mother hurried up to the deck where one of the ship's officers was waiting.

"I'm sorry we caused you so much trouble," Mrs. Bobbsey said to him.

The officer held up his hand. "I am the one to apologize. We would never have sailed if I had not thought all the passengers were aboard. Mr. Hansen told me he had seen you and your children return to the ship."

This statement amazed the Bobbseys. Back in their staterooms again, Bert called to Nan, "Why do you suppose Mr. Hansen would say that?"

"It sounds as if he wanted the ship to leave without us," Nan replied thoughtfully, "but I can't imagine why!"

Bert reminded his sister that Mr. Hansen had been talking with the Bobbseys' driver.

"Goodness!" Nan said. "You think old Striped Cap told him to make us late?"

Bert shrugged. "I wouldn't be surprised."

Later, at dinner, Karen Smith told the twins that she and her mother had not seen much of St. Thomas. "Mommy got a letter from Daddy which made her feel very sad. He said that one of his very best-carvings had been stolen. A famous artist in Kingston made it."

"That's too bad," Flossie said sympathetically. "Maybe Freddie and Nan and Bert and I can find it when we get to Jaca."

As the children left the dining room Bert noticed an announcement on the bulletin board. There was to be a costume party the next night.

"Goody!" cried Flossie. "I love to dress up!"

"I'll go as a pirate," Bert said at once.

"What can Freddie and I be?" Flossie asked.

Nan thought a minute. "How would you two like to go as an elephant?"

Flossie clapped her hands. "Yes! I'll be the front and Freddie can be the tail part!"

Freddie nodded eager agreement.

The next morning the twins enlisted the help of the room steward and Mrs. Bobbsey. Albert brought materials and costumes left over from previous parties.

Nan picked out a large piece of dark gray cloth. Then with her mother's assistance she sewed it up to form a body and four legs. Next she made an elephant's head of cardboard to cover Flossie's blond curls. One length of rope, fastened at the back, served as a tail while another was fixed to hang from the paper head as the elephant's trunk!

Giggling, the younger twins stepped into the cloth legs and scampered around the room. Freddie wagged the tail and Flossie made the rope trunk wave up and down.

Bert wore a pair of dark shorts, a white sport shirt, and wrapped a red scarf around his waist. A false mustache and a black eye patch provided the finishing touches.

"What are you going to be, Sis?" Bert asked.

Nan looked mysterious. "I'm a thermometer," she said, "but you can't see me until I'm ready."

Nan worked busily by herself all afternoon. The others did not see her in her costume until they were set to join the fancy dress procession to the lounge.

"Oh, Nan, you're bee-yoo-ti-ful!" Flossie exclaimed as Nan walked into the corridor.

"Very clever!" Bert said admiringly.

His twin had begged an old sheet from Albert. She had sewed this into a tight, straight garment which covered her from head to ankles. Up the middle of the white cloth she had painted a red line crossed with a series of straight black lines. She wore red shoes, and a black scarf around her head.

The judges were the captain and two of the passengers. The contestants marched past the platform at the end of the big room where the audience sat. There were all sorts of costumes—Spanish dancers, ghosts, babies, clowns, and many others.

Bert stalked past the judges, brandishing a blunt knife like a cutlass. Freddie and Flossie, as the elephant, capered along, tail and trunk waving madly, and Nan walked by, hardly moving a muscle. When all the masqueraders had paraded, the judges held a long conference.

Finally one of them stood up. "We have had a hard time coming to a decision, but we are awarding the prize for the most original costume to Nan Bobbsey, the thermometer, and the prize for the funniest to Freddie and Flossie."

There was loud applause as the three children came up to accept the prizes. Nan received a little red leather coin purse. Freddie and Flossie were given hats with the ship's name on the visor.

About noon the next day the *Jamaica Queen* pulled up to the Kingston dock. When the Bobbseys reached the foot of the gangplank a sun-tanned man came up to them. He was of medium height with very dark hair and brown eyes.

"Peter Henderson," he said with a pleasant smile. "I'm sure you must be the Bobbseys."

There was loud applause as the three children came up to
accept the prizes

Mrs. Bobbsey shook hands with the man and introduced the children. Then he led them to a slender blond woman who stood with a girl about Nan's height. She wore her dark hair in two pigtails down her back.

"I'd like you to meet my wife and our daughter Jennifer," their host said.

When greetings had been exchanged Bert looked around the pier. "Where's Phil?" he asked.

The smiles left the Hendersons' faces. "Our son has disappeared!" his father replied.

"How dreadful!" Mrs. Bobbsey exclaimed. "When did this happen?"

Mrs. Henderson explained that Phil had been missing since the previous afternoon. He had taken his little sailing boat out and had not returned.

"But Phil is an excellent sailor and the weather has been good, so we're sure he couldn't have had any trouble with the boat. The police are looking for him, and we're confident he'll be found soon," she concluded bravely.

"Oh, we hope so!" Nan said for her family.

The Hendersons had a large station wagon, and everyone piled in. The three girls sat together. "I hope you twins ride bikes," said Jennifer as they drove along. "We rented some for you to use while you're here."

"Oh, yes," Nan spoke up. "We all ride."

A short time later the car turned into a driveway and stopped in front of a pink stucco house. The first floor was level with the ground. An outside stairway led to a porch which surrounded the second story.

"This is an old Jamaican-style house," Mr. Henderson told his guests. "The first floor was formerly used for storage, but it is so cool that we have our living room and dining room there. The bedrooms open off the porch upstairs."

"It's lovely," Mrs. Bobbsey exclaimed.

Luncheon was served in the dining room, but with thoughts of the missing Phil, the meal was a somber one. Afterwards the children went out on the lawn. "Jennifer," Bert said, "could you tell us what Phil's pirate mystery is?"

Jennifer nodded. "It may have something to do with his disappearance," she replied.

She told the twins that Phil had been exploring a cave on Henderson Island, where her father conducted his sailing school. Phil had found an old scabbard. He had taken it to the museum and the curator had said it was probably the sheath for a pirate's sword.

"Phil thinks there may be treasure hidden on the island. You see, the pirates moved their headquarters from Ile de la Tortue to Port Royal, which is very near here."

"Wowee!" Freddie cried. "That *is* exciting!"

All the twins listened intently as Jennifer went on, "After Phil found the scabbard his picture was in the newspaper. About that time strange things began to happen on our island—I think he wrote you about the trouble with Daddy's boats."

Bert nodded. "Maybe Phil went back to Henderson Island," he suggested, "to do some more investigating."

"We thought of that," Jennifer said, "but the police went there today and couldn't find him."

The next morning when the twins came to breakfast Jennifer said that her father had gone off with the police to search the Jamaican coast in the opposite direction to Henderson Island.

"I'd still like to look for Phil on that island," Bert declared.

"We can," Jennifer said eagerly. "I know a man who will take us over in his boat."

Mrs. Henderson agreed that the older children might go to the island since Mrs. Bobbsey and the younger twins had been invited to lunch by Karen Smith and her parents.

After packing a lunch, Bert, Nan, and Jennifer set out on their bicycles. When they reached the waterfront Jennifer went up to an elderly man who was mending a fishnet. She asked if he would take them to Henderson Island.

The fisherman looked at Bert and Nan. "Are they the Bobbsey twins?" he asked Jennifer.

"Yes," she replied, surprised. "Why?"

"Well, I don't know as I want them in my boat," the man said slowly. "I hear they're trouble-makers!"

Bert and Nan stared at him. "Where did you hear such a thing?" Nan asked. "We only got here yesterday!"

"Oh, I heard it," was his reply.

Jennifer was indignant. "The Bobbseys are our guests and very nice people!"

The fisherman would not tell who had made the remark. But finally, with a shrug, he agreed to take the children in his outboard motorboat. When they arrived at the island, he climbed out, tied up his boat, and resumed work on the net.

The three children jumped ashore. "Let's walk along the water and look for signs of Phil," Bert proposed.

They made their way slowly, peering at the sand in hope of finding footprints. Nan was ahead. Suddenly she bent down and pulled aside the foliage of a large bush. There, concealed under the greenery, was a sailboat, made of a flat piece of wood with no sides. The sail lay beside it.

Jennifer came up behind Nan. "That's Phil's Sailfish!" she cried.

# CHAPTER VII

## THE HIDDEN PAPER

BERT raced up to the two girls and cried out, "If that's Phil's boat, he must be on this island!"

Nan nodded. "Since he hid his boat here, he must have walked inland from this point!"

"Phil! Phil!" Jennifer called. There was no response.

"Come on!" said Bert. "Let's find him!"

The three children picked their way through the underbrush and over the rocks of the small island, calling Phil's name. Still no reply.

Suddenly Jennifer stopped. "Listen!"

As she and the twins stood still, a faint cry reached their ears. "Help! Help!"

"It's Phil's voice!" Jennifer exclaimed.

"He's over there!" Bert turned and hurried toward a rocky hillside. The cries grew louder as the children approached it.

"Looks like the entrance to a cave there to the right," Bert said.

"Here I am, just inside!" a boy's voice called.

Jennifer dashed forward. Then, stooping, she entered the cave. "Oh, Phil! I'm so glad we found you!" she cried. "Here are Nan and Bert Bobbsey."

By the light sifting into the cave entrance Bert and Nan saw a boy seated on the ground. His face and arms were tanned and his blond hair bleached by the sun. When Phil got slowly to his feet, the twins saw that he was tall.

"Hello there," he said, and added ruefully, "Never thought we'd meet *here* for the first time, Bert." Phil winced with pain and slumped to the ground.

"You're hurt!" Jennifer said in dismay.

"I slipped on the rocks Thursday. I think I've sprained my ankle."

"That's a shame," said Nan. "And you must be starved!"

"I sure could eat." Phil grinned.

"We'll have lunch right now," said Jennifer.

Phil crawled from the cave, which he said had served as a shelter since his mishap. On a level spot nearby, Jennifer and Nan unwrapped the sandwiches while Bert poured cupfuls of milk from the thermos flask.

Phil ate and drank eagerly. When he had finished one sandwich, Jennifer urged, "Tell us all about what happened, Phil."

The boy said that he had sailed his Sailfish to the island on Thursday afternoon to search for possible pirate treasure. Shortly after he had landed a man arrived in a motorboat.

"He looked like an odd character, and I knew he had no business on our island. I hid my Sailfish and began to follow him. He seemed to be looking for something."

Phil went on to explain that while tracking the strange man he had wrenched his ankle.

"Lucky this cave was near enough for me to crawl into," said Phil. "I don't know where the man went. He probably took off in his boat."

"Didn't you hear the police calling you yesterday morning?" Bert asked.

Phil shook his head. "I must have been asleep. I didn't hear anyone until Jennifer called."

"Can you walk if you put your arm around my shoulders?" Bert asked.

Leaning heavily on Bert, Phil managed to hop down to the fisherman's boat. Its owner was waiting impatiently.

Jennifer and Nan hurried to get the Sailfish, and placed it in the larger boat. Then they all took off for Kingston. When they reached town, Bert hailed a taxi, put his bike in back, and drove home with Phil while the girls rode their bicycles.

While all this had been happening, Mrs.

Henderson had driven Mrs. Bobbsey and the younger twins down to the business district of Kingston. She dropped them off at a straw market.

"Mr. Smith's shop and home are just down that next street," their hostess said. "The shop is called *The Wood Basket.* You can't miss it."

Mrs. Bobbsey thanked her and followed Freddie and Flossie into the market. Many of the handmade straw articles hung on the walls. "What attractive hats!" exclaimed the twins' mother.

The hats were wide-brimmed with little woven figures and flowers of straw around the crowns. Flossie picked out one which suited her, then Mrs. Bobbsey selected a hat for herself and one for Nan.

"Oh! See the pretty dolly!" Flossie exclaimed, picking up a small doll made of cloth. The figure was a Jamaican girl in full skirts carrying a big water jug on her head.

"You may have the doll if you like, Flossie," her mother said, "and I think it would be nice to buy one for Karen."

Freddie chose a straw horse for himself and a pair of sandals for Bert. Then the twins and their mother turned toward the Smiths'. They found that the shop and house adjoined each other. Both had brilliant purple bougainvillea vines growing on them.

"It's bee-yoo-ti-ful!" Flossie cried.

Karen ran to meet them and introduced the callers to her father. Mr. Smith was a short, plump man with a worried expression. This vanished, however, as he and Mrs. Smith welcomed their guests cordially.

"Have the police caught the bad man who stole your carvings?" Flossie asked.

Mr. Smith told her sadly that no clue had been found which might lead to the thief.

"Would you like to see my shop?" he asked. "I'll show you some work done by the artist who made the stolen carving."

Mrs. Bobbsey and the twins followed their host through a passageway into an attractive showroom. On the walls hung pictures of Jamaica painted by local artists. Tables and shelves held wooden and stone figures.

Mrs. Smith picked up a wood carving of two children. "This was done by our most famous sculptor, Donald Dawson. He always signs his work like this." Mr. Smith turned the figure upside down and showed the Bobbseys two triangles cut into the bottom.

"The triangle is the Greek sign for the letter D," the shop owner explained.

"I see!" Freddie piped up. "D. D. for Donald Dawson!"

"That's right," Mr. Smith said with a smile. Then he picked up another piece. It was the figure of a Jamaican farm woman carrying a basket of fruit on her head. "This is my most valuable piece of Dawson's work."

"Ooh!" cried Flossie in wonder. "She looks so real!"

Karen had been listening intently to her father. Now she turned as her puppy Ginger came running into the room. "Ginger!" she scolded. "You know you're not supposed to come in here!"

The cocker spaniel pranced away from Karen's outstretched hand. Then he caught sight of the lacy straw hat which Flossie held. With a playful bark, Ginger grabbed the hat and ran through an open doorway.

"Catch him!" Karen cried. "He's going into the stockroom."

Flossie, Freddie, and Karen raced after the little dog. He tore around the small room and finally dashed beneath a table. He dropped the hat and crouched down, growling playfully, as if daring the children to come and get him!

Flossie crawled under the table on her hands and knees. As she picked up her hat, Ginger noticed a piece of newspaper lying on the floor.

With a playful bark, Ginger grabbed the hat.

The cocker snatched the paper in his teeth and pranced out into the room again.

Freddie finally caught Ginger, took the paper from the dog's mouth, and stuffed it into a pocket.

"You're a naughty puppy," Karen said sternly as she picked up the squirming cocker and carried him back into the shop. A few minutes later Mrs. Smith announced that lunch was ready.

When they were seated at the table, Mrs. Smith served portions of what looked like scrambled eggs.

"We thought you'd like to try a native Jamaican dish," she explained to the Bobbseys. "This is *akee,* made from the fruit of the *akee* tree which grows on the islands of the West Indies."

The younger twins thought the *akee* rather tasteless, but ate it politely.

"We have mangoes for dessert," Karen told them. "You'll like them!"

Flossie and Freddie found the slices of golden yellow fruit delicious. "They taste sort of like peaches," Flossie observed.

The children played during the afternoon and finally went back to the Hendersons. Freddie pulled a collection of articles from his pockets, including the piece of newspaper. As he started to throw it away, his attention was caught by the picture of a boy.

"That looks like the picture Phil sent to Bert," he thought.

Running into the living room where the grownups were talking, he showed the paper to Mrs. Henderson.

"This is Phil," she agreed, and sighed. "The article here is the one which appeared after he found the pirate scabbard."

Freddie wondered why the newspaper had been left on the floor of Mr. Smith's neat, orderly stockroom. Before he had a chance to mention this, a taxi drew up in front of the house. In a moment Bert got out, grabbed his bicycle, and then came toward the house with Phil leaning on him.

"Phil!" cried his mother. "Oh, thank goodness you're back safe!"

Amid happy confusion Phil was helped into the house and introduced to Mrs. Bobbsey and the small twins. As he was telling them and his mother the story of his adventure, Mr. Henderson walked in, closely followed by Nan and Jennifer.

Mr. Henderson examined his son's ankle and pronounced it a sprain. "You'll have to stay off your foot," he directed and bound up the ankle. "As soon as the swelling goes down, you'll be all right."

The dinner table that night was a lively one

with the six children chattering busily, comparing life in Jamaica and the United States.

Later, when Phil had been settled on a sofa with his leg propped up, the talk returned to pirates. "I'd like to see the scabbard you found," Bert said.

"It's on the book shelf in my room," Phil replied. "Why don't you bring it down?"

Bert and Freddie were sharing Phil's room, and Bert had already noticed the shelf which contained many of Phil's treasures. He ran up the outside stairway and quickly returned with the old scabbard.

The sword sheath was made of heavy leather reinforced by metal bands. The children gathered around to examine it.

"Too bad the pirate's sword wasn't there too," Bert remarked as he ran his fingers over the scabbard. Suddenly he stopped, a puzzled expression on his face. "It feels as if there's something in the tip!"

He passed the scabbard to Phil, who felt the end of the sheath. "I say! It does! Let's open it!"

Mrs. Henderson brought a sharp knife from the kitchen, and Bert finally succeeded in slitting one side of the small tip. He pushed a finger in carefully. "There *is* something here!" he cried. The next minute Bert pulled out a folded piece of parchment!

# CHAPTER VIII

## NIGHTTIME THIEF

THE children crowded around Bert to see what he had found in the scabbard tip. Carefully he unfolded the parchment. The creases had turned brown and the paper seemed ready to crumble into bits. Its surface was covered with a fine, spidery writing.

Flossie jumped up and down in excitement. "What does it say, Bert?" she asked impatiently.

Bert carried the paper over to a lamp and looked at it. "I can't read this," he said finally. "The words are spelled queerly."

Mr. Henderson took the parchment and spread it out on the table. "It's old English writing," he explained. "The s's look like f's."

The message read: *Capt. Browne difpofed of. Treafure in cave on my turtle, not hif. J. Morrif.*

"Oh!" cried Nan, "do you suppose the Capt. Browne was Casey Browne's pirate relative?"

She told Phil and Jennifer about the seaplane pilot and his search for treasure.

"But how could there be a cave on a turtle?" Jennifer asked with a little giggle.

They discussed the strange message for some time but still could not fully understand it. Finally Bert decided to take the parchment to the museum after church the next morning.

"I'm sorry I can't go with you," Phil said, "but Mr. Masters, the curator, is a nice chap and will give you his opinion about this find."

As Phil had predicted, the curator was very much interested when Bert showed him the old parchment. "This is extremely important!" Mr. Masters said, carefully putting the message down on his desk. "I hope you will let me keep it here in the museum. We will take steps to preserve it."

Bert explained that the parchment really belonged to Phil but that he felt sure the boy would agree to its being kept in the museum.

"You know," Mr. Masters said thoughtfully, "this may solve the mystery of what became of Captain Henry Browne and the treasure he was supposed to have captured from a Spanish galleon. I think there was also a buccaneer named John Morris. Morris may have stolen the treasure from Browne and hidden it."

"But what about the turtle?" Bert asked.

The curator told him that Ile de la Tortue

north of Haiti had also been known as Tortuga
Island. The pirates used the island for their
headquarters for many years until they moved to
Port Royal. "Tortuga is the Spanish word for
turtle," he concluded.

"Then perhaps 'my turtle, not his' means the
treasure is hidden on another turtle-shaped island," Bert suggested.

"That could well be," Mr. Masters agreed.

Phil listened eagerly when Bert told him what
the curator had said. "We'll have to find that
other turtle island!" he declared solemnly.

That night Phil and Freddie were sound
asleep when Bert suddenly awakened. He lay
quietly for a moment, trying to figure out what
had aroused him. Then all at once he froze.

*A shadowy figure was standing by the book
shelf!*

Before Bert could make a move the figure
snatched something from the shelf, ran out onto
the porch and down the outside stairway!

Bert leaped from his bed and dashed over to
the book shelf. The scabbard was gone!

"Phil! Freddie!" he called as he started for the
porch. "A thief has taken the pirate scabbard!"

The other boys sat up sleepily, then Freddie
jumped to the floor. "Stay in bed, Phil!" he
shouted. "I'll get the robber!"

Bert, followed by Freddie, dashed down the

A shadowy figure was standing by the book shelf!

stairs and out toward the street. At the end of the driveway Bert collided with a man.

Then in the glow of the street light Bert saw the man's face. "Casey Browne!" he exclaimed. "What are you doing here? Did you see anybody run from this house just now?"

Casey edged away. "No, I didn't," he said quickly. "I'm in a hurry." With that, he hastened off down the street.

The Bobbsey boys were astounded. "Why didn't Casey stay and talk to us?" Freddie asked. "He acted awful funny."

Bert turned back to the house. "I don't know. I guess he had something very important to do." The pilot's strange behavior was forgotten in the excitement of calling the police and describing the burglary to them.

Later when the boys were in bed again, Phil spoke up. "It's a jolly good thing we found that parchment message before the scabbard was stolen! Otherwise we wouldn't have the clue to the treasure."

Bert agreed. In another minute all three boys were fast asleep.

The next morning Bert rode his bicycle to the library. He intended to read all he could about the pirates who had lived in Jamaica.

When he asked the woman at the desk if he might use the books she asked his name, then called the head librarian.

"You're Bert Bobbsey?" the elderly man asked. When Bert nodded, the librarian looked undecided. "We've had a report that you make a nuisance of yourself," he said.

For a moment Bert was speechless. Someone was apparently going around telling untrue stories about the twins! Who? And why?

"I don't understand this," Bert said finally. "I'll promise to be quiet."

The elderly librarian relented. "You may use this library, young man, but you must treat the books carefully."

Bert said nothing more beyond a polite "Yes, sir." In the history section he found a book about the pirates of the Caribbean. Something he read there made him hurry back to the Henderson house.

Phil was stretched out in a hammock on the lawn when Bert rode in. "Any luck?" he called.

Bert hurried over to him. "I found something which gave me an idea," he said. He told Phil that Henry Morgan, one of the most famous buccaneers, had once had a house near Port Maria. "If we could go there, perhaps we'd find a clue to the pirate treasure."

Mrs. Henderson and Mrs. Bobbsey were seated nearby. "Port Maria is on the north coast of Jamaica," their hostess said to Mrs. Bobbsey. "You really should see that area."

After some discussion, it was decided that next morning Mrs. Bobbsey would borrow the Hendersons' large convertible and drive the children to the north coast for a few days' visit.

"I hope your ankle will be better by tomorrow, Phil," Mrs. Bobbsey said. "I'd like to have you and Jennifer go with us."

"I'm sure I'll be tops by then," Phil assured her with a grin. "I can walk better now."

When morning arrived Phil found he could get around again almost as well as ever. Everyone was ready to leave when Bert suggested calling police headquarters about the stolen scabbard. He talked to an officer who said so far not a single clue had been found. Then the children and Mrs. Bobbsey started out in the early morning coolness. As the car left the city and traffic behind, the children noticed many Jamaicans walking along the road.

"They're bringing their fruits and vegetables to sell at the market," Jennifer explained when Nan pointed to several women who balanced broad baskets piled high with produce on their heads.

"This is a magnificent drive," Mrs. Bobbsey commented as the narrow road wound higher and higher up into the mountains. On first one side of the road and then the other there were deep ravines filled with tall bamboo trees.

"Wait until we get to Fern Gully," Jennifer told her. "It's near Ocho Rios. It's spooky!"

The road continued on its twisting course through the mountains. Suddenly the group found themselves on a stretch of road bordered by almost vertical high banks. On these banks grew giant ferns which made the road so dim it seemed to be passing through a tunnel.

"This is the famous Fern Gully," Phil said.

Nan shivered in the sudden coolness. "I see what you mean about its being spooky, Jennifer," she said.

A short while later Mrs. Bobbsey turned onto the road which ran along the north coast. A few miles farther on she drove into a private lane leading to a long, low pink stucco building and parked.

"Mrs. Henderson made reservations for us here at the Jamaica Inn," she told the children. "It's right on the beach so we can swim."

"It's bee-yoo-ti-ful!" Flossie cried as they walked through a breezeway. A green lawn stretched from a terrace surrounding the inn down to a beach of dazzling white sand.

The Bobbseys and the Henderson children were shown to three rooms opening off the terrace. Each one had its own private porch.

When they had unpacked they all walked to the other end of the terrace where luncheon was being served. They were given a table beside a stone balustrade.

The long ride had made the children hungry, and they were soon enjoying the tasty food. Suddenly Flossie put down her fork. "Look!" she whispered, nodding toward the railing.

There was a little green lizard about four inches long stretched out on the stone top. As they watched, the lizard raised its snake-like head and a fold of orange skin ballooned under its neck.

"Isn't he pretty!" Flossie exclaimed.

"That's a chameleon," Jennifer told her. "We have lots of them in Jamaica—sometimes for pets."

"I'm going to have this one for a pet," Flossie decided. She watched the chameleon carefully as she finished her ice cream. The little animal seemed unafraid and eyed the group steadily.

When they were ready to leave the table, Freddie reached over and gathered the tiny creature up in his hand. "I'll carry him for you, Flossie."

"I'll call him Jimmy," Flossie said.

While the older children hurried to change into swimming things, Freddie and Flossie played with Jimmy on the porch outside the room which Mrs. Bobbsey and Flossie were using.

"Let's go to the beach, too," Freddie said when the others started down.

"We can tie Jimmy to a chair while we're gone," Flossie proposed. Freddie agreed.

They got a piece of silk thread from Mrs. Bobbsey's sewing kit, carefully slipped a loop around the lizard's neck and tied the other end to the leg of a chair. Then the small twins put on bathing suits and scampered down to the water.

Some time later Freddie and Flossie ran back to the terrace. "Let's see how Jimmy is," Flossie suggested and hurried toward the chair.

"He's gone!" she wailed.

The little chameleon had slipped his head out of the loop of thread and escaped!

"Maybe he's still around," Freddie said and began to search the porch. Then he walked into the bedroom.

"Jimmy's here, Flossie!" Freddie called. He pointed to a picture which hung over Flossie's bed. The lizard lay along the top of the frame.

"I'll get him!" Flossie climbed onto the bed and stretched up her arms. But the frame was too high and the bed was soft. A second later Flossie lost her balance.

She grabbed the picture to steady herself. It came off the hook, and Flossie and the picture bounced from the bed onto the floor. The chameleon scurried from the room!

# CHAPTER IX

## A SPOOKY HOUSE

"FLOSSIE!" cried Freddie. "You let Jimmy get away!"

"I couldn't help it," Flossie wailed. "And I've hurt my knee!"

Freddie hurried over and helped his twin to her feet. "I'll get you a sticky bandage," he volunteered.

He ran into the bathroom and returned with an adhesive plaster which he put over the scratch on Flossie's knee.

"Thank you," she said. "I'm sorry about Jimmy, but maybe he'll come back."

Next morning the waiter brought them all breakfast on Mrs. Bobbsey's porch.

"What a nice way to serve oranges," Nan said as she picked up a fork on the end of which was skewered a whole peeled orange.

"This is the Jamaica way," Phil explained.

"They're easy to eat." He showed her how to nibble the fruit.

At that moment a little yellow bird alighted on the table and pecked at a crumb of toast. Flossie put out her hand, and the bird hopped onto it. The little girl wrinkled her nose. "He tickles!" she said, giggling.

"It's a banana bird," Jennifer told her. "We call them that because of their color."

When everyone had finished breakfast, Bert stood up. "How about going to Port Maria this morning? Maybe we can find out where Henry Morgan's house was."

Mrs. Bobbsey agreed, and in a short while they were on their way. The drive along the ocean was pleasant although the Bobbsey children found it hard to get used to the cars driving on the left side of the road.

"I hold my breath every time a car comes around a corner toward us," Bert confessed.

They passed many natives striding along, carrying heavy bundles on their heads. One woman at the side of the road, evidently waiting for a bus, made them laugh. Set solidly on the top of her head was a small can of tomatoes!

Finally, after riding through several sleepy-looking villages, they arrived at the outskirts of Port Maria. Nan pointed to the ocean. "Look!" she said. "There's a seaplane just taking off."

"It looks like Casey Browne's!" Bert exclaimed. "That's a skull and crossbones on the fuselage!"

"Is he looking for pirate treasure?" Freddie piped up.

"Could be," Bert said. "I wish he'd come and see us. He promised to."

Bert again wondered about the pilot's haste the other evening and the reason for it. By now the travelers had reached the square in the center of Port Maria.

"Where do you want to start your search for Henry Morgan's place?" Mrs. Bobbsey asked.

"I'll go in that drugstore and ask if anyone knows where it is," Bert volunteered.

Mrs. Bobbsey parked the car and Bert walked over to the store. The door was standing open. As Bert stepped inside, a man pushed out past him. The man was thin and had a dark complexion. Bert noticed a white scar over his left eye.

In reply to Bert's inquiry, the proprietor of the store told him that nothing was left of the Morgan place.

"The people around here think that it was up in the hills south of Port Maria. There are two pillars of rock which are supposed to mark the place where the house used to stand."

Bert thanked the proprietor and turned to leave. "What's up?" the druggist asked him.

"That fellow you passed on your way in was asking me the same question."

"Nothing special that I know of," Bert replied. "I'm just interested in pirates and wanted to see where Henry Morgan lived."

Following Bert's directions, Mrs. Bobbsey drove out of town and turned south. They were soon in mountainous country again. The road was narrow, dusty, and steep. Fortunately they met only a few cars, but these came around the sharp corners at full speed.

"Goodness!" Nan gasped. "I hardly dare look!"

The children kept watching for the twin rocks. Finally a short distance to one side, Freddie spotted two rocky pillars rising above the green bushes and small trees. "There they are!"

Mrs. Bobbsey applied the brakes and pulled the convertible as far off the narrow road as she could. They all got out. Freddie and Flossie ran across, with their mother close behind them. Nan, Jennifer, and Phil followed.

Bert lagged behind a bit, then started to cross. As he stepped into the road an old car whizzed past, narrowly missing him!

"Hey!" Bert yelled. "Slow down!"

By this time the car had disappeared around a sharp bend. "That's funny," Bert said when he joined the others. "The driver of that car was

A car whizzed past, narrowly missing Bert.

the man who asked the druggist in Port Maria about Henry Morgan."

"There was another man with him," Phil remarked. "But he was crouched down in the seat, so I couldn't see what he looked like."

"He should never drive at that speed on these twisting roads!" Mrs. Bobbsey said indignantly. "He almost hit you, Bert!"

Her son grinned. "But he missed! Let's look for any signs of Henry Morgan's place."

The six children, followed by Mrs. Bobbsey, picked their way through the thick underbrush. The walking was difficult, but they finally managed to reach the two tall rocks.

"I don't see anything," Flossie remarked, disappointed. "I thought we were going to a pirate's house!"

"It isn't here any more, honey," Nan explained, "but we'll look for clues to show us where it was. Maybe he lived in a cave!"

The children walked carefully around the rocks, peering to see if they could find parts of a foundation or a cave. But there was nothing. They searched around the base of trees for any signs of buried treasure, without success.

Nan wandered off a little distance to admire the view over the valley. As she started back toward the others she suddenly stumbled against a large, flat stone and fell to her knees.

She got to her feet and examined the stone. It appeared to be one of several. As she looked farther, the young detective discovered a line of stones overgrown with weeds and partly sunk into the ground.

"Bert!" she called. "Come see this."

Her twin hurried over. When Nan showed him what she had discovered he walked along the line of stones. "This might have been the foundation of Henry Morgan's house!" he guessed. "It would be a good idea to dig under these stones. There might be treasure hidden here!"

At that moment Mrs. Bobbsey called, "Bert! Nan! I think it's going to storm. We'd better get back to the car."

Bert and Nan looked up at the sky. Instead of the beautiful blue which it had been earlier in the day, it was now covered with dark clouds. A stiff breeze had sprung up.

"It does look like a storm," Bert agreed, "but I hate to go."

The twins dashed back across the road to the convertible. "We'll put the top up," Jennifer and Phil told Mrs. Bobbsey.

But though they struggled hard they could not get the mechanism to work. The top stubbornly refused to rise!

"Get in the car," Mrs. Bobbsey urged. "I'll drive on a little way. Maybe we can find shelter."

She drove as fast as she dared on the narrow, winding road, peering from side to side for sight of a house. The wind grew stronger and the sky darker.

"There's something up ahead!" cried Freddie. "I think it's a house."

But when they arrived at the building, they found it was in ruins. The place had evidently been a large mansion at one time, but now most of the roof had fallen in, and where doors and windows had been there were only gaping holes.

"There's still part of a roof in the back," Bert pointed out.

Mrs. Bobbsey drove the car under a tree, and they all got out. As they ran toward the house, the rain started to come down in torrents.

Finally, soaked and out of breath, the little group reached the shelter. This section of the mansion had withstood decay better than the rest. The walls were streaked, the floors were full of holes and there was no glass in the windows, but at least there was a roof!

"Goodness," said Mrs. Bobbsey as she tried to wring water out of her dress. "I hope this doesn't last long."

"It's a tropical storm," Phil assured her. "They're pretty violent but they're usually over quickly."

"This is spooky," said Flossie, looking around the dim room. "I don't like it!"

"We're lucky to be inside," Nan said comfortingly, "and we won't be here long."

The rumble of thunder had come nearer, and now there were regular crashes. With this and the sound of the heavy rain against the walls, it was almost impossible to hear what anyone said.

They all sat down on the floor in the corner of the room farthest from the rain and waited. It seemed hours. Then suddenly the rain stopped and the thunder died away. As Mrs. Bobbsey and the children started to get to their feet, they heard a loud sneeze!

Someone was in the next room!

# CHAPTER X

## THE PEACH STONE MONKEY

"WHO'S that?" whispered Flossie, her blue eyes wide with fright.

Bert started toward the next room of the crumbling mansion. "Wait!" his mother said quietly. Before she could say anything more, they heard the sound of running feet.

The older children raced outside. They were just in time to see their convertible speeding down the road!

Nan gasped and Bert cried out, "Well, how do you like that? Now we *are* stuck!"

"Who could have been in that ruined house?" Nan asked. "And what was he doing there?"

No one could answer her questions. They walked back to tell the others what had happened. They were shocked.

Freddie spoke up. "Boy! I wish we could catch him!"

"That's not possible now," Bert told him. "But let's look around these rooms. We might find some clue to the person who was here."

The sun had come out, so the searchers were able to see more clearly. The group walked around slowly, looking for anything unusual.

Freddie stalked ahead, his hands behind his back, peering at the floor. Suddenly he stooped and picked up something from a corner.

"See what I've found!" he called, holding out his hand. In it lay a peach stone monkey!

"Just like Casey's!" Nan exclaimed. "Do you think it's his?" she asked in bewilderment.

At the small twins' urging, the pilot had shown his lucky piece to Bert and Nan on the ship, and they in turn had told Phil and Jennifer about it.

Now all the children gathered around Freddie to peer at the carved peach stone. Did it mean that the pilot had been in the ruins? If so, why?

"Put the monkey in your pocket, Freddie," Bert directed. "When we see Casey, we can ask him."

Before Freddie's call Phil had been examining something in another corner of the room. Now he went back to it. "There's a hole here," he said. "Looks as if something had just been dug out of it."

"Whoever we heard in this room must have done that," Bert said. A startling thought occurred to him. "Was it Casey? And what had he found?"

"I don't believe the person was Casey," Nan stated. "We saw his seaplane take off from Port Maria."

The children examined the rest of the ruined house without finding anything else of interest. Finally, at Mrs. Bobbsey's urging, they left the place and began to walk along the road.

The area appeared to be deserted. There were no houses in sight and no cars came along. Then the bushes and weeds at the side of the road gave way to a neat planting of wide-leaved stalky trees.

"Here's a banana grove!" Phil cried. "There must be some sort of house around."

Peering from side to side, the party walked on. Then, in a little clearing they saw a small thatched-roof shack. An elderly man was seated in front. He straightened up and bowed gravely as Mrs. Bobbsey and the children left the road and walked over to him.

"Our car has been stolen," Mrs. Bobbsey said. "I wonder if you could help us. We want to get back to Port Maria."

The man pointed proudly to a big old-fashioned automobile parked under a tree a short distance away. The car had lost most of its paint and blended into the landscape so completely that the children had not noticed it.

"I can drive you to Port Maria," the farmer said with a broad smile. "My automobile is old, but it still runs!"

"Oh, wonderful!" Nan said gratefully.

The twins' mother and the six children piled into the roomy car, and the man started down the road. The motor ran smoothly and quietly.

. They had just reached the end of a steep hill and turned a corner when Nan called out, "There's our car!"

The convertible was at the bottom of a small slope at one side of the road. The farmer stopped. They all got out and ran down the incline. The automobile seemed to be undamaged.

"I think I can drive it up," Mrs. Bobbsey said thoughtfully. "You children direct me."

She slipped behind the wheel and started the motor. It came to life quickly. "Tell me when to turn," she called to Bert and Phil, who stood near the front of the car.

But the recent rain had soaked the ground, and when Mrs. Bobbsey put the car into reverse and tried to back up the incline, the rear wheels spun helplessly.

"Stop, Mother!" Bert told her. "You're digging the tires into the mud. We'll have to get something to put under them."

The children hurried into the underbrush and came back with armloads of dried palm branches. These they packed behind the rear wheels.

"Try again, Mother," Bert directed, "and give it plenty of gas!"

Mrs. Bobbsey put the car into reverse once more and pushed down on the acclerator. With a spurt which scattered the dried pieces of palm, the tires took hold and the convertible lurched up the slope onto the road.

"Hurray for you, Mother!" Flossie cried, clapping her hands. "You're a good driver!"

Mrs. Bobbsey insisted upon paying the farmer for his trouble, then drove back toward the inn. On the way everyone discussed the mystery of the stolen convertible.

"It wasn't really stolen," Nan pointed out. "Whoever took this car didn't want to keep it— he just wanted to leave us stranded."

Bert shook his head, puzzled. "I don't get it," he admitted. "Who would want to do that?"

They reached the inn in time for a very late lunch. Afterward, Mrs. Bobbsey rested on her porch, while the children went down to the beach. It was bordered by several tall coconut palms.

"I'm going to sit in the shade," Flossie announced, settling herself against the base of one of the trees which had a sloping trunk. The others flopped down in the warm sand, and soon all of them were asleep.

Suddenly there was a *thump* close beside Flossie's head. She awoke with a start. On the sand lay a big coconut!

"Did it hurt you?" someone asked.

Flossie jumped up and stared at a native boy about eight years old. He looked at Flossie with friendly brown eyes. He wore faded blue shorts and a worn white shirt. His brown feet were bare.

When Flossie shook her head, the boy pointed to the tree. "I was picking some coconuts," he explained, "when one of them dropped. I was afraid it might have hurt you."

During this conversation Freddie had awakened. "You mean you climbed that tree?" he asked the boy in surprise. "The branches are so far up, how can you *climb* it?"

The boy gave Freddie a big grin. "My name is Johnny," he said. "I gather coconuts for the cook. I'll show you how."

As Freddie and Flossie watched, Johnny ran up the sloping tree trunk like a monkey, grasping the smooth bark with his hands and toes.

"That looks easy," Freddie said. "I can do that." He slipped off his sandals, dashed to the tree and managed to get a short distance up the trunk.

Then he stopped, his hands and feet clinging to the bark. He could move neither up nor down. Finally he let go and fell to the soft sand with a grunt.

By this time Johnny had reached the top of the tree where the coconuts were clustered. He pulled off two and scrambled back down to the beach. He handed the fruit to Freddie and Flossie.

"One of the waiters at the inn will open them for you," Johnny said. "The milk inside is good—so is the meat."

"We have coconut cake sometimes," Freddie remarked, "and that's awful good."

With a wave Johnny ran off. Freddie and Flossie took the coconuts to the inn, where one of the maids promised to see that they were opened. That night at dinner there were tiny glasses of coconut milk at each place and a bowl of crisp white slices.

"Mm!" Flossie chewed a piece of the coconut meat. "This is yummy!"

The next morning at breakfast, Mrs. Bobbsey asked, "What would you children like to do now? We won't start back to Kingston until after luncheon."

"It would be fun to take a trip on the White River," Phil suggested. "It flows into the ocean

Freddie could move neither up nor down.

just a little way up the beach. We can get a canoe from the inn."

Freddie and Flossie decided they would rather play on the beach, and Mrs. Bobbsey said she would stay with them. Phil spoke to the manager and soon one of the hotel employees brought a canoe to the beach. Bert and Phil took the paddles while Nan and Jennifer sat on the bottom in the middle of the craft.

With Phil pointing the way, the boys paddled around a point of land and followed the shore a short distance. Then they came to the mouth of the White River and turned into it. The tropical stream was narrow, and the high growth on either side made it shady. The water was deep green.

"This looks like a real jungle!" Nan exclaimed as she watched the scenery slide past. Both banks were covered by thick undergrowth. There were tall palm trees whose huge fronds almost met overhead.

"This is a lonesome place." Jennifer shivered.

"We're not the only ones on the river," Nan said. "See, there's a man in a canoe."

Bert peered ahead in the gloom. "Say!" he exclaimed. "That man's wearing a striped cap. Do you suppose it's Mr. Hansen from the ship? I'd like to ask him some questions."

"See if you can catch up to him!" Nan urged.

The boys began to paddle harder. They were

narrowing the distance between the canoes when the man glanced back. Immediately he increased his speed.

"Hurry, Bert!" Nan cried. "He's turning into a side stream! We'll lose him!"

Bert and Phil did their best. The canoe sped along. When they reached the smaller stream, the man was nowhere in sight. Phil swung the canoe into the narrow passage.

Here the growth was even thicker, and it was almost dark. The tropical waterway wound in and out among the jungle trees.

After a few minutes Phil stopped paddling. "We'd better not go any farther," he said. "We don't know what's ahead. It may be dangerous."

"I guess you're right," Bert agreed.

The two boys swung around and began to paddle back to the main river. They had almost reached the turn when Jennifer suddenly pointed to the nearby bank above them. "That fallen log just moved!" she said in a choked voice.

Phil looked over. "That's not a log! It's a crocodile! Paddle faster, Bert!"

At that moment the reptile slid into the water with a splash. His head hit the canoe, which teetered dangerously.

Nan screamed!

# CHAPTER XI

## NAN'S DISCOVERY

WHEN the crocodile struck the canoe, the four children quickly grasped the sides to balance it. The water rippled gently behind them as the reptile swam off in the opposite direction.

"Oh!" Nan gasped in relief. "I thought we were going to tip over and fall into the water with that horrible creature!"

"I guess he was as scared as we were," Phil remarked with a grin. "At least he got away fast!"

As they paddled back toward the mouth of the river, Bert said regretfully, "We'll probably never know whether or not that man was Hansen!"

Freddie and Flossie were envious when they heard the story of the crocodile. "I wish I'd been there," said Freddie wistfully. "I'd have hit him on the head with the paddle!"

The others laughed, and Bert rumpled his little brother's hair affectionately.

The trip back across the island to Kingston that afternoon was uneventful. Mr. and Mrs. Henderson welcomed them warmly when they arrived at the pink stucco house.

Later, after all the adventures had been related, Mrs. Henderson turned to Flossie. "I forgot to tell you that Karen Smith phoned and would like you to ring her."

Flossie ran to the phone and dialed the Smiths' number.

"Oh, Flossie!" Karen cried when she came to the phone. "Something terrible has happened!"

"What's the matter, Karen?" Flossie asked.

"Do you remember the Jamaican woman carrying the basket?"

Flossie thought a moment. "You mean the D. D. statue?"

"Yes! Somebody stole it from my daddy's shop last night!"

"How awful! Did the police catch him?"

"No, and Daddy can't understand how anyone could get into his shop."

Karen went on to explain that in an effort to stop the robberies, her father had put new locks on all the doors. There had been no sign that any of them had been broken.

"It's very strange," Flossie agreed.

Flossie told her family and the Hendersons the story. They felt very sorry for Mr. Smith.

The next day Phil asked the Bobbseys, "How would you like a swim on this side of the island?"

When they all agreed this was a good idea, Mrs. Bobbsey offered to drive them to a beach east of Kingston. She explained that Mrs. Henderson would be busy during the day and had suggested that Mrs. Bobbsey use her car.

"I want to buy some gifts for our friends at home," the twins' mother said. "I can take you children to the beach. When I come back you may go in the water."

"Let's have a picnic," Jennifer proposed.

"Goody!" Flossie said. "I'll help fix it."

All the children ran to the big kitchen and with Mrs. Henderson's help made sandwiches, cut cake, and poured milk into thermos jugs.

Finally everything was ready. The children put on their swim suits, took towels, and drove off with Mrs. Bobbsey. When they reached the beach and Flossie caught sight of the clear blue water, she remarked, "The deep blue sea is all around Jaca, isn't it?"

"Of course," Bert said teasingly. "That's what makes it an island!"

Mrs. Bobbsey stopped the car, and the children jumped out. They made their way down the steep bank to the white sand.

"I brought a ball," Phil said when they reached the beach. "We can have a game."

The six children formed a circle and began to throw the ball from one to another. After a while they decided to toss it at random, trying to take one of the others by surprise. This caused a good deal of laughing and shouting.

"Throw it to me!" Freddie pleaded. But, teasingly, Phil tossed the ball to Nan. Then, when Freddie was not looking, Nan threw it to him.

The little boy saw the ball coming but too late. Before he could put up his hands, it had gone past him, hit the sand and rolled into the water. The next moment a wave broke and, in receding, carried the ball out to sea.

"I'll get it!" Freddie called and ran into the water. But the ball bobbed farther and farther away. He started swimming after it.

"Freddie, come back!" Nan called. "Mother told us not to go in the water!"

But her brother did not hear her. In his desire to get the ball back, he forgot his promise and kept on swimming. Nan dashed to the edge of the beach, made a shallow dive and swam out to Freddie. She reached him and told him to forget the ball. The two were turning around when they heard a loud whirring noise above.

Looking up, the children saw a helicopter

hovering over them. A man leaned out the window and motioned them to go ashore. As they hesitated, he frantically waved again toward the beach.

"Come on, Freddie!" Nan cried. "He wants us to get out of the water! I wonder what's the matter!"

The other children had been watching with wide-eyed interest. "What was that all about?" Bert asked as the two swimmers came ashore.

Nan shook her head in bewilderment. "I don't know," she replied.

The next moment Flossie pointed down the beach. "He's landing!" she cried out.

With a whirring of its rotors the helicopter settled down on the wide stretch of beach. The children dashed toward it.

A man jumped down to the sand. He was Casey Browne!

"Casey!" Freddie cried, reaching the pilot first. "Why are you flying a copter?"

"And why did you want us to hurry out of the water?" Nan asked.

"Hi, kids!" the blond young pilot said with a grin. "I didn't know it was you Bobbseys swimming. I was cruising along here when I saw a barracuda in the water. They can be pretty nasty—I didn't want you to get hurt."

"They're really dangerous fish," Phil agreed.

"Come on, Freddie!" Nan cried. "He wants us to get out of
the water."

"Thank goodness they don't often come inside the reef."

Bert introduced Casey to Phil and Jennifer. The pilot explained that he had come to Kingston to see his friend who owned the helicopter. "He lent it to me while my seaplane is being overhauled."

Nan was about to mention the seaplane the twins had seen when Bert said, "We have a lot to tell you, Casey." He described Phil's discovery of the ancient scabbard, and their finding of the parchment message in the tip.

" 'Captain Browne disposed of,' " Casey repeated the words thoughtfully. "I wonder if he was my ancestor, Henry Browne. It sounds as if this J. Morris stole the treasure and hid it on some island."

"That's what Mr. Masters at the museum thinks," Bert agreed excitedly.

"Perhaps I should stop looking for wrecked ships and start hunting for an island!" Casey remarked with a grin.

"We think it must be a turtle-shaped one," Nan put in eagerly.

"By the way, Casey," Bert spoke up. "Were you in Port Maria on Wednesday?"

When Casey hesitated, Nan explained, "We thought we saw your plane taking off as we were driving into town."

The pilot told them he had flown up to Port Maria on business that day but had not stayed long.

Flossie's eyes strayed to the small pocket in Casey's slacks. The pocket looked very flat, as if the peach stone monkey was not inside.

"Did you lose your little peach monkey?" she asked. " 'Cause maybe Freddie found it."

Casey did not reply. A disturbed expression came over his face, and he looked away from the children. Before the twins could question him, the pilot said in a relieved tone, "Here comes your mother."

When Mrs. Bobbsey had greeted the pilot he made a suggestion. "How would you all like a ride in the copter?" he asked.

The twins had traveled in a helicopter one summer from their Uncle Daniel's farm near Meadowbrook to visit their Cousin Dorothy at Ocean Cliff. They liked riding in a whirlybird.

"Oh, yes!" Flossie jumped up and down. "Let's go!"

"That would be keen," Phil said excitedly. "Jennifer and I have never been in a copter."

Mrs. Bobbsey smilingly agreed, and Casey helped the children into the aircraft. A few minutes later it rose straight up, then turned and flew inland.

The children pressed their noses to the windows to watch as the craft passed over Kingston.

"There's our house!" Jennifer exclaimed as she spotted the pink stucco building and the green lawn around it.

When the town had been left behind, Casey turned the copter along the shore once more.

"Show us your island," Freddie urged Jennifer as they came within sight of several small patches of land off the coast.

"There it is." Jennifer pointed to one of the larger islands. They all craned their necks to see.

"It's shaped like a turtle!" Nan explained in astonishment.

Bert gave a joyful shout. "Maybe that's the island J. Morris meant!"

"I say!" Phil looked down. "We never realized the shape of our island."

"Can we land, Casey?" Bert asked eagerly. "We could explore."

The pilot shook his head. "Sorry," he said. "I don't see a good landing spot down there. Besides, I must take this chopper back to my friend."

The children were disappointed, but they accepted Casey's decision. He slowly turned the helicopter around and flew back to the bathing beach. They thanked him and hopped out. He gave a friendly wave and lifted his craft off the beach. A few minutes later it was off into the blue sky.

"Wasn't that 'citing!" Flossie exclaimed.

"It made me hungry," Freddie announced.

Bert and Phil brought the picnic basket from its hiding place behind a palm tree. Nan and Jennifer quickly spread out the array of sandwiches, fruit, and cake. Mrs. Bobbsey filled the cups with milk.

As the children ate hungrily, they discussed the surprising discovery that Henderson Island from the air appeared to be shaped like a turtle.

"Wouldn't it be keen if the treasure should turn out to be buried on our island?" Phil said.

"We must explore right away!" Bert proposed.

"I wish Casey could have landed on it," Freddie spoke up.

Bert looked thoughtful as he munched his sandwich. Then he said slowly, "Do any of you think that Casey acts sort of—strange?"

Nan nodded. "Yes, he does."

# CHAPTER XII

## THE WARNING

"WHAT'S odd about Casey?" Jennifer asked with interest.

"I don't know exactly," Nan said slowly, "but he appears in places suddenly and doesn't seem to want to tell us why."

"Remember, he was walking past your house, Phil, the night the burglar stole the scabbard," Bert said. "And he was in such a hurry he didn't even wait to hear what had happened."

"He admitted he was in Port Maria on Wednesday," Nan went on, "but he acted, well, almost scared, when Flossie asked him if he had lost his peach stone monkey. There must be some explanation," she added hopefully. "I'm sure Casey is really a nice man."

That evening at the dinner table the children told Mr. and Mrs. Henderson that their turtle-shaped island might be the hiding place for the pirate treasure.

"We'd like to go there and search," Phil told his father.

"We could camp out while we're treasure-hunting," Jennifer suggested.

"Say, Jen, that's a good idea!" her brother said. "May we do that?" He looked eagerly at his parents.

"I don't see why you four older children shouldn't camp there," Mr. Henderson said. "After all, the short-wave wireless in my office shack on the island is connected to police head-quarters in Kingston. Phil knows how to work it if anything should happen."

"And there's the signal flag we could run up in case the wireless didn't work," Jennifer added.

Mrs. Bobbsey and Mrs. Henderson looked at each other doubtfully. "Would you be willing to stay with them for one night, Mary?" Mrs. Henderson asked. "I'd feel better if a grownup was there."

Mrs. Bobbsey nodded. "I think that's a good idea, Eunice. Richard and I often camp out with the twins, and I enjoy it."

"Are you going without Freddie and me?" Flossie asked, her blue eyes beginning to fill with tears.

Mrs. Henderson leaned over and patted the little girl's hand. "Mr. Henderson and I need some children to stay with us," she said with a smile. "We will think of something extra special for you to do while the others are away."

"Okay," Flossie and Freddie agreed reluctantly.

Next morning Phil told the Bobbseys that they were to sail over in the Hendersons' sloop, the *Hibiscus*. "She's really keen," he added. "You'll like her!"

When all the supplies had been gathered together, Mr. Henderson drove the campers to the dock, where the *Hibiscus* was anchored. She was a trim vessel, having a white hull with a red stripe, and red and white striped sails.

"You don't need to worry," Mr. Henderson said to the twins' mother. "Phil and Jennifer are both excellent sailors."

"I'm sure they are," Mrs. Bobbsey replied with a smile. "Bert and Nan love to sail, too. Perhaps they can be of some help."

It was a beautiful, sunny morning with a steady breeze blowing. When everyone was settled in the *Hibiscus* Nan gave a sigh of contentment. "I'm ready for another adventure on the deep blue sea," she said.

"Me too!" Bert grinned.

With the good breeze and Phil's expert handling of the sails, the *Hibiscus* reached Henderson Island in twenty-five minutes. Phil tied up at the small dock, and his passengers jumped ashore.

Jennifer told the Bobbseys that the island was about half a mile long and a quarter of a mile wide. It was thickly wooded with silk-cotton, breadfruit, and palm trees and broken up by a good many low hills and deep gullies. Like the rest of Jamaica, the soft limestone was full of caves.

Near the dock stood a small shack which served as Mr. Henderson's office when the sailing school was in session. A short distance away an area had been cleared and a number of tents set up for use by the students.

Mr. Henderson had left the tents standing, hoping the mystery of his damaged boats would soon be solved. Mrs. Bobbsey chose a tent and deposited her bag. Nan and Jennifer put theirs in the next tent and the boys took one on the other side of the clearing.

"Let's eat before we start exploring," Phil suggested.

Mrs. Henderson had provided the campers with a picnic lunch, and supplies with which to cook supper and breakfast.

When they had eaten and cleared away the debris, Mrs. Bobbsey did not feel it necessary to explore with the children and said she would remain on the dock and read. "I'll be right here if you want me."

The twins and their friends set out. "Show us the cave where you found the scabbard, Phil," Bert urged.

"Okay."

Phil led the other three through the woods until they came to a rocky ridge sparsely covered with bushes. "This ridge is full of caves," he told them. "I think the one the scabbard was in is about here."

Phil searched among the bushes, pushing the branches aside, until he found an opening. "This is it," he called.

He pulled out a flashlight and beamed it into the entrance. "Do you want to go in?"

"Sure!" Bert replied. "Maybe the treasure was hidden right in here with the scabbard."

Each of the children had brought a flashlight. They turned them on now as they crept through the narrow opening.

Bert shone his light around in a wide arc. "Someone else has been here!" he exclaimed. "Look at those footprints!"

The dry dirt on the floor of the cave was covered with prints. As the children bent to examine them, they saw that some had been made by heeled shoes while others appeared to be flat sandal prints.

Phil looked worried. "Whoever it was came after I did," he said. "I wonder if the person found anything."

"Maybe the strange man you saw discovered this cave," Bert guessed.

The four made their way forward as far as they could, examining the ground, sides, and top carefully. But they could see no signs that anything had been removed, so they came out again.

During the afternoon they tramped over a good part of the island without finding a trace of any treasure or intruders.

"I guess we may as well give up for today," Phil said finally in a discouraged tone.

"Who's for a swim before supper?" Bert asked.

"Me!" the others chorused and they hurried back to the tents. A few minutes later the four children were splashing around in the cool blue water. They had short races and diving contests. Each one won two of them.

Jennifer laughed. "USA against Jamaica is a tie!"

When it was almost dark Phil and Bert built a fire. Mrs. Bobbsey and the girls prepared the supper of steaks, fried potatoes, and sliced tomatoes with juicy mangoes for dessert. Afterward they sat around the fire for a little while watching the moon rise over the water, then went to bed.

Some time later Nan was awakened by the

sound of men singing. Startled, she sat up in her sleeping bag and listened. Who could they be? She crawled from the bag and crept to the door of the tent. As she stood there trying to hear the song more clearly, Jennifer came to stand beside her.

"Let's see who it is," Jennifer whispered.

When the two girls reached the center of the clearing they saw Phil and Bert leave their tent. A moment later Mrs. Bobbsey sleepily joined them.

"Do you know who is singing, Phil?" she asked.

"No," the boy replied. "No one else is supposed to be on the island."

"It sounds like pirate songs," said Bert after straining his ears to hear the words.

"Pirate songs!" Jennifer shivered. "Where would the pirates be?"

"I'm going to find out!" Phil started to walk in the direction of the singing.

"We'll all come with you," Mrs. Bobbsey insisted.

She and the four children crept to the edge of the clearing. Suddenly the singing stopped. They waited breathlessly, but the sound did not begin again.

Mrs. Bobbsey turned back. "We'll go back to

bed. In the morning we'll find out where the singing came from."

The thought of pirates excited all the campers, and it was some time before everyone dozed off. Nan awoke early the next morning, dressed quickly, and went outside. As she started to walk toward the boys' tent to wake them, she stopped short and stared. In the center of the cleared area a dagger had been stuck into the ground! It was holding down a sheet of paper.

"Bert! Phil!" she cried. "Come out here! Hurry!"

Jennifer, the two boys, and Mrs. Bobbsey popped from their tents. Nan pointed to the dagger and paper. "Where do you suppose that came from?" she asked in a shaky voice.

"Something is written on the paper," Bert said.

He stooped and picked up the dagger. Nan pulled off the paper and looked at it curiously. There was a crude drawing of a skull and crossbones at the top. She read the message aloud.

LEAVE THE ISLAND AT ONCE. YOU ARE DISTURBING THE SPIRIT OF HENRY MORGAN!

"How weird!" said Mrs. Bobbsey.

Nan remarked, "I guess whoever wrote this

A dagger had been stuck into the ground!

doesn't know we're looking for J. Morris's treasure, not Henry Morgan's."

"And I think it proves," Phil added, "that he doesn't know about the message we found in the scabbard."

"Let's see if we can find out where the singing came from last night," Jennifer proposed. "Maybe that would give us a clue as to who wrote this warning."

After a hurried breakfast Mrs. Bobbsey and the children started off. They made a complete tour of the island, looking for signs of a campfire which the men might have built. They found nothing. The island seemed peaceful and deserted.

Finally the searchers made their way back to the tents. Nan, curious about the dagger, picked it up. The dagger was about eight inches long. Its handle was wooden and carved with fruits and flowers. As she turned the dagger over in her hand Nan noticed that the tip of the handle was flat. She looked at it more closely.

Carved into the wood were two tiny triangles. Greek D's!

# CHAPTER XIII

## TING AND LING

NAN stared at the dagger handle. "This was made by the famous artist, Donald Dawson!" she cried out.

Jennifer and the boys crowded around to see the weapon.

"Wowee!" Bert exclaimed. "I wonder if the dagger was stolen from Mr. Smith's shop!"

Phil was excited. "If it was, this proves that the same person who has been stealing things from the shop is also trying to find the pirate treasure!"

"Let's take the dagger to Mr. Smith," Nan proposed, "and find out if it does belong to him."

"We may as well," Phil agreed. "We haven't been able to discover anything else here on the island."

In a short while they had cleaned up the camp, and were once more sailing the *Hibiscus* toward

Kingston. When they reached the dock Mrs. Bobbsey hailed a taxi to drive them to *The Wood Basket*.

Karen was playing in the garden and followed the children into the shop. Mrs. Bobbsey went on to the house to see Mrs. Smith.

At once Nan showed Mr. Smith the dagger and told him where they had found it. He looked astonished.

"I have a list of stolen articles," he said. "Let me see if this is one of them."

He went into his office and returned with a typewritten sheet. While the children watched eagerly he ran his finger down the columns.

Suddenly Mr. Smith stopped. "This is it," he said. "One eight-inch dagger, wooden handle carved by Donald Dawson."

"Then we have a good idea that the thief was on our island last night," declared Phil. "He was probably one of the 'singing pirates.'"

"If we could only catch him, or find the treasure before he does!" Nan said worriedly.

"You twins seem to be pretty good detectives," Mr. Smith remarked. "I'm glad to have this dagger back. Maybe you can find the rest of the stolen articles."

All the children promised to try. They said good-by and joined Mrs. Bobbsey. "If you'll drop me at the museum," Bert said when another taxi arrived to take them to the Hendersons, "I'd like to talk to Mr. Masters again."

"Right-o," Phil replied. "We'll see you at the house."

The curator seemed pleased to see Bert and led the boy into his office. Bert told him about their visit to Port Maria and their discovery that Henderson Island was shaped like a turtle. "But we haven't been able to find a clue to pirate Morris's treasure," he concluded.

Mr. Masters became thoughtful. "Many years ago," he said, "there was a man here in Kingston who made a study of pirates and their activities. In fact, he located some of the hidden loot. He was a descendant of one of the earliest settlers of Jamaica."

"Could I talk to him?" asked Bert eagerly.

Mr. Masters shook his head. "He has been gone a long time. But he did have a son, who is very old now and rather eccentric. You might be able to get some help from him. He may have papers of his father's which would shed light on Henry Browne or J. Morris."

"Where could I find him?" Bert asked.

Mr. Masters said the man's name was James Bennett and he lived up in the Blue Mountains outside of Kingston. He gave the boy directions for reaching the house. Bert thanked the curator and hurried off. The Henderson and Bobbsey families were just sitting down to a late lunch when Bert arrived. He told them what he had learned.

"If you don't mind driving again, Mary," Mrs. Henderson said, "you might take the children out to Mr. Bennett's. It's beautiful up in the Blue Mountains."

Mrs. Bobbsey said she would enjoy the trip, and in a little while she and the children set out. Kingston was quickly left behind as they rode up into the mountains.

At the top of a steep rise she pulled the car into a lookout space, and they all admired the view. Far below, the buildings of Kingston clustered at the edge of the blue sea. Tiny dots of white sails could be seen on the water, and a plane was coming in for a landing at the airport.

"It's bee-yoo-ti-ful!" Flossie exclaimed.

Mrs. Bobbsey drove on. The road wound higher. Presently Bert called out, "That must be the place." He pointed to a small wooden house on the side of the mountain. The back of it nestled against the slope while the front was approached by a long flight of steps.

The car was parked in a small level spot. Then, with Bert in the lead, the callers climbed the steep steps. Bert knocked on the door. In a few minutes it was opened part way by a small old man with a white beard.

"Are you Mr. Bennett?" Bert asked.

The beard wagged assent. "Come in, come in," the man said in a high, squeaky voice. He opened the door a bit wider. "Hurry, please, or Ting and Ling will get out."

Quickly the Bobbseys, Phil, and Jennifer squeezed through the opening. Inside they found a room jammed with furniture. The two small windows were covered by draperies.

When the visitors' eyes became accustomed to the dim light they saw two beige-colored cats, with brown heads and tails, clinging to the curtains. Suddenly one threw itself from the drapery and leaped onto the top of a nearby chest. The other cat followed.

"What pretty kitties!" Flossie cried, running up to try to pat one. The cat squirmed from her hand.

"I call them Ting and Ling," Mr. Bennett explained. "They're Siamese cats and not very friendly to strangers."

Bert introduced his mother and the others. "We've come to ask you about pirates," he began.

At that moment the first cat jumped from the chest and landed on the elderly man's shoulder. He put up his hand and gently stroked the creature's tawny fur. "You must be good, Ling," he said. "Our visitors want to talk to me."

As if he understood Mr. Bennett's words,

Ling leaped from his shoulder. The cat jumped up on the chest and took its place beside Ting. The two pets sat quietly, watching the children.

Bert began to explain their mission to the elderly man. Freddie meanwhile looked around the room. His eyes fell on a little brown mouse peeping from under a couch. The little boy watched for several seconds. The mouse did not move.

"I think I can catch it," the little boy told himself. He noticed an open paper box on a table. Quietly Freddie picked up the box and crept toward the couch. Then with a pounce he clapped the box over the mouse.

"I've got you!" he cried triumphantly.

The others looked around, startled. Mr. Bennett began to laugh. "You've caught Ling's plaything!" He chuckled. "Raise the box and see."

Freddie lifted the box a little and peered cautiously under it. The mouse had not moved! It was a toy!

With a sheepish grin, Freddie picked up the mouse and put it on the chest where the two cats were seated. Immediately they began to bat it back and forth.

When the laughter over Freddie's mistake had died down, Bert again turned to Mr. Bennett. "We thought perhaps your father had left

Freddie lifted the box and peered cautiously under it.

some sort of records which would tell about any pirate treasure hidden around these islands."

Mr. Bennett's blue eyes twinkled as he looked at the children. "Well, I'll tell you. My father had a very close friend. He used to talk to him all the time. This friend must be almost a hundred years old. He once lived with me, but he left because he just couldn't get along with the cats."

"Do you know where he is now?" Bert asked in excitement. "Could we go see him? Your father might have told him what he knew about pirates."

Mr. Bennett smiled. "The Skipper, as we always call him, lives over in Spanish Town at Mrs. Tucker's."

"What is his address?" Phil asked. "We could drive over there tomorrow."

Still smiling broadly, the elderly man gave Phil the address. Then the callers left.

The next day, when the Hendersons and their guests were having lunch Mr. Henderson spoke to his son. "Your mother and Mrs. Bobbsey tell me they're going to a party this afternoon. Is there any place you'd like to take the twins?"

"Yes, Father," Phil replied. "Would you drive us over to Spanish Town? An old man we want to talk to lives there."

"By all means," Mr. Henderson agreed. "The

Bobbseys should see Spanish Town. It was the capital of Jamaica in 1872."

"I'll take my Jaca dolly," Flossie said. "She'll like to see it."

Spanish Town proved to be a small, dusty village. Mr. Henderson took them to the main plaza which was surrounded by mellowed old stucco buildings. These had once been government offices. In the center of the plaza was a park shaded by many palm trees.

"We'll have to ask where Mrs. Tucker's house is," Phil reminded his father.

"I hope Skipper remembers about the pirates," Freddie remarked. "Mr. Bennett said he was awful old."

Phil's father drew up to the side of the street where several small boys were playing ball. Phil jumped out and ran over to them.

When he came back he told his father the address was that of a restaurant. "The boys said it was just behind the Rodney Memorial." He pointed to an imposing white building with a red tile roof.

The restaurant was not hard to find. It was a neat-looking place with several tables set out in front.

"I hope Mr. Skipper is still here," Jennifer said as her father parked the car in the shade of a tree.

"You children go in," Mr. Henderson suggested. "I'll wait for you in the car."

The restaurant was empty when the six children walked in. A revolving fan in the ceiling made a soft whirring sound.

"I say," Phil called, "is anyone here?"

In reply a young woman came through a doorway at the rear of the room. "I'm sorry," she said, "dinner won't be ready until seven."

"We're looking for Mr. Skipper," Nan spoke up. "Does he still live here?"

The woman looked puzzled. "Mr. Skipper?" she repeated.

"Yes," said Bert, "Mr. Bennett told us we would find him here with Mrs. Tucker. We'd like to ask him some questions."

A smile spread over the woman's face. "I'm Mrs. Tucker," she said. "Yes, Skipper is in back."

As she opened a door at one side of the room, the children heard a hoarse voice say, "Hello!"

"This is the Skipper!" Mrs. Tucker announced.

# CHAPTER XIV

## THE GHOST TREE

THE children pressed forward eagerly. There was no one in the room! Then again they heard a hoarse "Hello."

"It's a parrot!" Nan exclaimed. She pointed toward a brilliant red-and-green bird swinging on a ring in front of the window.

"But where is Mr. Skipper?" Freddie asked, bewildered.

Mrs. Tucker laughed. "This is the Skipper," she said.

"Mr. Bennett told us the Skipper was an old friend of his father's," Jennifer said, still not understanding.

"Mr. Bennett loves a joke," Mrs. Tucker explained. "I suspect he was playing one on you!"

She went on to tell them that the elder Mr. Bennett's favorite companion had been the parrot. He had talked to him constantly.

"But after old Mr. Bennett died, the Skipper couldn't get along with Mr. James Bennett's cats. They bothered him so much that Mr. Bennett sent Skipper over here. He has been with me ever since."

As the children turned to leave, the Skipper called out, "Good-by, pirates!"

Disappointed though they were, this made the youngsters giggle. "Good-by, Skipper!" Flossie replied, running from the room.

Mr. Henderson laughed when they told him about the parrot. "It's too bad you didn't find out what you wanted to, but think what a good time Mr. Bennett had fooling you!"

"He sort of reminds me of a boy at home named Danny Rugg," Bert said ruefully. "Danny's always playing tricks."

"I think there's a place down the street where they have good lemonade," Mr. Henderson said. "Would that make you feel better?"

"Yes, Dad," Jennifer cried. "We'd all like some."

The drink refreshed them. Afterward, the children strolled past a row of shops. In one window Flossie noticed a carving of two kittens.

"They look like Ting and Ling," she declared. "Maybe I can buy them for Mommy."

"That's a good idea," said Nan. "The boys and I will help you pay for it."

The twins went into the shop and asked to see the carving. "It is an unusually fine one," the shop owner said as he hurried to take it from the window. "I've had it only a few days."

The man handed the carving to Flossie. It showed two kittens seated side by side eying a ball of string.

"Aren't they darling?" Flossie exclaimed as she ran her fingers over the lifelike figures. "Look at their tails!" She turned the carving over to show Nan.

Her sister peered at it closely. "Oh! This is by Donald Dawson!" she exclaimed. "See the two triangular Greek D's on the bottom!"

"Did you buy these kittens from Mr. Dawson?" Flossie asked the shop owner.

"Never heard of him," the man answered.

"Where *did* you get the carving?" Nan persisted.

The owner said he had bought the figure a few days before from a child who had brought it into the store.

"The boy said he had found the carving. He wanted to sell the piece so I bought it. That's all!"

"We're interested in finding out where the boy got it," Bert explained. "Do you know him?"

"Sure," the man said. "He runs errands for me once in a while. His name is David Hawkins. He lives just off the road to Kingston in a shack at the edge of a big sugarcane field."

The twins pooled their money and paid the man for the carving, then followed Phil and Jennifer from the shop.

"Let's look for David right now," Flossie urged as they walked toward the car. "Maybe he knows who took the things from Karen's daddy."

When Mr. Henderson heard the story he agreed to stop at the Hawkins place if the children could locate it. Soon the car came to a sugarcane field. The passengers kept a sharp lookout on both sides of the road for a shack at the edge of the field. They passed several little dwellings, but no one was around them. "Everybody's probably away cutting sugar cane," Phil said.

Finally Freddie cried, "There's a house! And I see a boy in front of it!"

The shack was a little larger than the others they had passed. An extension of the thatched roof was supported by four poles, forming a sort of sheltered porch. A boy of about eight sat on the ground leaning against one of the poles. He was chewing on a piece of sugar cane.

Mr. Henderson stopped the car. Freddie and Flossie jumped out and ran across to him.

"Is your name David Hawkins?" Freddie asked him.

The boy's face lighted up in a big grin. "It sure is!" he replied. "You lookin' for me?"

Flossie held out the wooden carving. "Did you find this?"

The boy looked surprised but nodded.

"Where did you find it?" Flossie asked eagerly.

David pointed up the road. "By Cringle's Tree," he said. "But don't you go there," he added hastily.

"Why not?" asked Freddie.

" 'Cause it's haunted!" David replied, his eyes rolling with fright. "The duppies'll get you if you bother that old tree!"

"Are you sure it's haunted?" Freddie asked. "We don't believe in ghosts!"

David looked very serious. "Ever since I found those wooden cats on the ground under that tree, I've had nothin' but trouble," he declared. "I bought me a ball with the money I got for that carvin' and I lost it. Then I cut my toe so I can't run errands." He held up a bandaged foot.

"That's too bad, David," Flossie said sympathetically.

"Where is the tree?" Freddie asked.

"It's a big old silk-cotton down the road," the boy replied, "but I'm warnin' you, keep away from it!"

When Freddie and Flossie told the others what David Hawkins had said, Mr. Henderson smiled. He explained that the tree known as Cringle's Tree had been a landmark on the Spanish Town road for over a hundred years. Many stories had been written about the tree and the natives believed it was haunted by "duppies" or ghosts.

"That sounds interesting," said Bert. "Let's go and see it."

Mr. Henderson drove on. A short time later he pulled up beside an enormous tree. The twins gasped at its size.

"How big around is it, Mr. Henderson?" Nan asked.

"About fifty feet," he told her.

The children piled out of the car and ran over to look at the tree. "It's as big as a house!" Flossie cried. She gazed up at the lowest branches which were far above her head.

"I'm going to see if I can find any more statues," Freddie announced. He began to walk slowly around the huge tree base.

"I'll look, too," Phil declared. Soon all six were searching the ground beneath the old tree.

Freddie, who was in the lead, stopped suddenly when he reached the far side of the trunk. From this spot the road and traffic were completely hidden from view.

"Look!" he cried. "Someone's dug a deep hole here!"

The others ran around to see it. Close to the base of the tree was a large cavity which appeared to have been recently dug.

"And here are footprints!" Bert pointed out. "They were made by someone wearing sandals. There are no heel marks."

"Just like the prints we found in your cave, Phil!" Nan said excitedly.

"That's right," Phil agreed, "but it may not mean anything. After all, lots of Jamaicans wear sandals."

"Maybe something's down there." Flossie leaned so far over the hole, she started to lose her balance and threw out her arms to steady herself. The Jamaican doll which she had clutched under one arm fell into the hole!

"My dolly!" she cried. Flossie stretched out on the ground and reached down into the cavity.

In doing this, the little girl saw a key in the dirt near the doll. She reached farther and managed to grab the key. In a few seconds Flossie stood up, the doll in one hand, the key in the other.

"Look what I found!" she said proudly.

The other children gathered about her to inspect the key. "This may be a good clue!" Bert exclaimed. "If that cat carving is one of the

"Look what I found!" she said proudly.

things stolen from Mr. Smith's shop and it was buried here, then the key could be very important!"

"You mean it might be a key to *The Wood Basket!*" Nan cried.

"You Bobbseys are real detectives," Phil said admiringly.

"Let's go see if it fits!" Flossie cried, jumping up and down impatiently.

The children ran back to the car and piled in. "Did you like Cringle's Tree?" Mr. Henderson asked.

"Oh, yes!" they chorused.

Excitedly they told him of their discovery. "Please drive to Mr. Smith's shop, Daddy," Jennifer urged. "We *must* see if the key Flossie found fits his door!"

When they reached *The Wood Basket,* Mr. Smith was busy with several customers. Flossie ran over to the house to find Karen. In a few minutes she was back, hand in hand with the little dark-haired girl.

"Karen wants to see if the key fits," Flossie explained.

"We'd better wait until Mr. Smith is free," Bert remarked.

The children waited impatiently until the three tourists had made their selection of gifts and Mr. Smith had wrapped their packages. As soon as they left, the shop owner turned to his visitors.

"What can I do for you?" he asked with a smile. "You all seem excited about something."

Flossie showed him the carving of the kittens and explained where she had found it. Mr. Smith quickly identified it as one of the articles stolen from the shop. Then Flossie took the key from the pocket of her shorts and held it up.

"Does this fit your door?" she asked. "I found it in the hole by the big Cringle Tree."

Mr. Smith looked amazed. "What would my key be doing out there?" he asked. "I can't understand it."

Flossie ran to the gaily painted front door and slipped the key into the keyhole. It would not turn the lock!

"Oh dear," Nan groaned. "I was sure we had found a wonderful clue."

"Wait a minute!" Mr. Smith said. "All the articles stolen were taken from the stockroom. It has a back door."

The children dashed into the rear room. Once more Flossie put the key into the lock. It turned easily!

# CHAPTER XV

## AN L-SHAPED CLUE

"THE key fits!" Flossie cried happily.

Mr. Smith shook his head in bewilderment. "I still don't understand how the new key to that door could have turned up in a hole by Cringle's Tree!"

Karen's father explained that when he had decided to change the locks on his shop because of the burglaries, he had given the job to a locksmith in the neighborhood.

"Did you lose your key?" Freddie asked.

"No, it's always right here on my ring." Mr. Smith held up a bunch of keys and pointed to one. "This is it."

"Then someone had a duplicate!" Phil declared.

"Maybe the locksmith would know," Nan said.

"I'll ask him," Mr. Smith said grimly. "His place is just around the corner."

"May we go with you?" Flossie asked, her blue eyes bright in anticipation.

"Sure, come along," Karen's father said cordially. "After all, you found the key."

It was decided that Flossie and Nan would go with Mr. Smith. The others would wait in the car with Mr. Henderson.

Karen ran to the house to ask her mother to stay in *The Wood Basket* while Mr. Smith was gone. She hurried over, then the two girls set off with the shop owner.

The locksmith's place was on the next street. The proprietor, whose name was Patton, was alone when Mr. Smith entered with Nan and Flossie.

"A duplicate key?" Mr. Patton asked in surprise at the gift shop owner's question. "I didn't make any duplicates. I sold you one set of new keys, and the locks, which my assistant put on. That's all I know."

Mr. Smith showed him the key which Flossie had found under Cringle's Tree and explained that it fitted the storeroom lock.

The locksmith was puzzled. "I can't understand it," he said, "but I'll ask my assistant. He's working out back now."

He went into a rear room. The girls and Mr. Smith heard a low conversation. In a few minutes Mr. Patton returned. "Ken says he doesn't know anything about a duplicate," he reported. "It's a mystery."

Flossie gave a great sigh. "Nothing's going right."

The next morning after breakfast Mr. Smith telephoned Bert. "I just had a call from Patton," he said. "He tells me his assistant, Ken Clark, didn't come to work this morning and he hasn't heard from him. Patton thinks it may have something to do with that key Flossie found yesterday."

"Wow! I suppose you've reported this to the police?"

"I'm just about to do that, Bert. I'll let you know if anything more develops."

During the morning Bert and Phil discussed the case. "I'd like to talk to Ken myself," Bert said. "Let's get Nan and see if we can find him."

Phil jumped up from his chair. "Right-o! I'm with you, Bert. Where do we start?"

"First to the locksmith shop to see where Ken lives."

A few minutes later the two boys and Nan jumped on their bicycles and pedaled off. Mr. Patton told them that Ken lived in a rooming house almost across from the Myrtle Bank Hotel. "He doesn't have a telephone, so it's possible he is ill and isn't able to let me know."

The three rode on to the Myrtle Bank Hotel.

Across the street and down a short distance they saw a sign in the window of a shabby-looking house. It read: "Rooms for Rent."

"That must be the place," Bert said, jumping off his bicycle and propping it. "I'll see if Ken's here. If he is, I'll call you."

Bert ran to the house and knocked on the door. Nan and Phil watched eagerly as a woman opened it. They saw her shake her head and in a few moments Bert was back, looking discouraged. "The landlady says Ken moved out last night, and didn't say where he was going."

"That certainly sounds suspicious," Nan observed. Then she added, "Since we don't know where to look next, I have an errand I can do for Mother. She has ordered a dress to be made in a shop in the Myrtle Bank Hotel. I told her I'd ask how it's coming along."

"I'll go with you," Bert offered.

"You two go ahead," Phil suggested. "I'll stay here and keep an eye on our bikes."

Nan took care of her mother's errand, then she and Bert started back across the street where Phil was waiting.

As the Bobbseys stepped into the road a boy on a bicycle whizzed past, barely missing the twins. They jumped back quickly.

The cyclist stopped beside a policeman who was directing traffic at the hotel entrance. Pointing back at Bert and Nan, he said loudly, "Father, those kids tried to make me fall off my bike! I'm sure they're the Bobbsey twins!" With that, he pedaled off down the street.

"How did he know us?" Nan asked, puzzled.

The policeman left his post and walked over to the curb where Bert and Nan were still standing. "Is that right?" he asked. "Are you the Bobbsey twins?"

"Yes, we are," Bert replied.

Nan added, "We certainly didn't try to make your son fall. He wasn't looking where he was going. He almost knocked us down!"

The officer eyed the children sternly. "We've been warned that you twins are troublemakers," he said. "I'll let you go this time, but watch your manners while you're in Kingston."

The twins were too astounded to reply. In a moment the policeman went back to his post and began to direct traffic once more.

"Wh-what was he talking about?" Nan asked her twin.

"This is the third time we've heard complaints about us," Bert replied. "One more thing to figure out."

That afternoon the twins, Phil, and Jennifer held a conference. "We're not getting anywhere with our two mysteries," Bert said glumly.

"That's right," Phil agreed. "We haven't

found one clue to the treasure J. Morris hid."

"And we promised Karen we'd find the bad man who stole her daddy's things, and we haven't!" Flossie wailed.

"What can we do?" Jennifer asked.

"I'd like to take another look at the message we found in the scabbard," Bert declared.

A few minutes later the six children were on their way to the museum. Mr. Masters welcomed them warmly. When Bert explained that they wanted to see the parchment message, he carefully took it from a drawer.

"It hasn't been on display yet," he said. "I'm waiting until we can have the paper treated to preserve it."

The curator laid the parchment on a table and weighted it down at each corner. One by one, the children bent over it, trying to find a clue to the treasure's hiding place.

When Nan's turn came, she picked up a magnifying glass which lay nearby. Through it, she peered at every word of the message. Nan was about to put the glass down when she suddenly paused.

"Here's a clue, maybe!" she cried.

Nan pointed to the word *cave*. "See those tiny lines under it?" she asked.

The others took turns peering at the spot. Finally they all agreed that the almost invisible

Nan peered at every word of the message.

lines formed an L with a horizontal line on each side.

"But what do they mean?" Flossie wanted to know.

The children thought hard, but no one could suggest a reason for the strange lines. Finally Nan said slowly, "Perhaps they mean that the cave is shaped like an L."

"Okay," Bert agreed, "but what about the other lines?"

Freddie spoke up. "They could stand for something sticking up on each side, like a tree or a big rock."

"Freddie and Nan, I think you're both right!" Bert exclaimed. "We must go back to the turtle-shaped island!"

# CHAPTER XVI

## MR. SHIFTY

"YOU'VE found a clue, Nan!" Phil cried.

"When may we go to the island and search again?" Nan asked excitedly.

Phil thought a moment. Then he explained that he and Jennifer had promised to play in a tennis match the next morning. "We can sail over there tomorrow afternoon, though," he said.

Bert and Nan went with Phil and Jennifer to watch the match. But Freddie and Flossie decided to ride to the Myrtle Bank Hotel with their mother while she had a fitting on her dress. In the courtyard in front of the hotel there were many shops that sold gifts of all kinds.

"If you two would like to look around here," Mrs. Bobbsey suggested, "I'll meet you in the hotel lobby when I've finished."

"I have an idea," Flossie said to Freddie as their mother left.

"What's that?" asked Freddie.

"Mommy says when you're visiting people, it's nice to give them something," Flossie declared. "So let's buy a gift for Mrs. Henderson."

"Say! That would be fun," Freddie agreed. He pulled several coins from his pocket. "I have twenty-five cents."

"Good!" said Flossie. She opened her little purse and carefully counted the money in it. "I have forty cents," she announced.

The first shop the twins entered turned out to have only wicker furniture. "That's a nice chair," Freddie observed.

Flossie looked doubtful. "I don't think we have enough money for that," she said.

The next shop they went into sold jewelry and perfume. But here, too, they found their money would not buy anything.

"There are lots of pretty things here," Flossie observed, peering into another store window.

Followed by her twin, Flossie walked into the shop. The shelves were filled with all kinds of native craft, including bags, baskets, and hats made of straw.

Freddie and Flossie looked at everything and finally decided on a set of straw coasters, for which they had just enough money. As they were leaving with their package, a thin, poorly dressed man entered. He asked for the owner.

Freddie and Flossie looked at him intently. The man wore sandals on his bare feet. A white scar stood out plainly over his left eye. In his hand he carried a carved wooden figure.

"Wait!" Freddie whispered. "He looks like the man who almost ran over Bert when we were looking for that pirate's house!"

The small twins watched as the man held up the carving to show to the shop owner.

"That's just like Karen's daddy's statue!" Flossie exclaimed. She dashed across the room to where the two men were talking.

"May I see that, please?" Flossie asked. She looked closely at the carving. It was the figure of a Jamaican woman with a tray of intricately carved fruits and vegetables on her head.

The thin man gave Flossie a startled look. Then he mumbled something and hurried toward the door, clutching the wooden statue.

At the door he collided with a man who was just coming in. The customer turned and stared after the thin man as he dashed up the street.

"What was *he* doing in here, Mr. Gordon?" the newcomer asked the proprietor.

"He wanted to sell me a wood carving, but he ran out when this little girl asked to see it. Do you know him?"

"Sure! I advise you not to have any dealings with him. He's a crook named Shifty Peters."

"May I see that, please?" Flossie asked.

Flossie looked up at the customer. "Do you know where Mr. Shifty Peters lives?" she asked.

The man nodded. "Just across the way." He led Freddie and Flossie to the door and pointed out the rooming house a short distance down the other side of the street.

"Why are you so interested in him?" Mr. Gordon asked Flossie in surprise.

She and Freddie told the shop owner about the thefts from Mr. Smith's shop. "And that lady with the basket on her head was stolen," Flossie concluded.

"I have heard about Smith's trouble," Mr. Gordon said. "I'll notify the police at once."

While he was making the call the other man left. But Freddie and Flossie decided to wait for the police. "Maybe we can help them," Freddie said importantly.

Before long a squad car with two officers drove up. They identified themselves as Green and Winton. When Mr. Gordon told them about Shifty Peters and the stolen carving, Green, the officer in charge, asked if he knew where the scar-faced man lived.

"We do!" Freddie piped up promptly.

The two policemen followed the small twins across the street and down to the shabby-looking rooming house. "This is the place," said Freddie.

The officers went up and knocked on the door. It was opened in a few minutes by a middle-aged woman. When the policeman asked to see Shifty Peters, the woman shook her head.

"He hasn't been here for several days," she said. "He told me he was expecting a friend from the States. I guess he's staying with him."

"Did Peters take his things when he left?" Officer Green asked.

"No, they're still in his room on the second floor," the landlady replied. "He took only a couple of packages."

"We'll look around," the officer declared, walking toward the stairs. Winton and the two Bobbsey children followed.

The landlady plodded up the stairs behind them and unlocked a door at the back of the second floor. They all went in.

The room was poorly furnished. There was a bed with a lumpy-looking mattress, a battered table piled high with newspapers, an old bureau with a cracked mirror, and a straight chair. A wardrobe stood in one corner.

The officers quickly inspected the room. "Nothing here," Winton observed.

Officer Green walked over and flung open the door of the wardrobe. An old suit and a torn raincoat hung from the rod.

Freddie was standing beside the officer. The

little boy leaned forward to peer into the closet. On the floor was a collection of rags. A dark object protruded from beneath them.

"What's this?" The little boy bent down and pulled it out. It was Phil's scabbard!

"What have you there?" Green asked.

Freddie's eyes sparkled. He told the officer about the theft of the scabbard.

"Well," the policeman commented, "it seems this Shifty Peters has stolen other things besides the carvings from Mr. Smith! We'll have to find him. I'll take the scabbard for evidence, but Phil can have it back soon."

Freddie suddenly remembered the newspaper clipping about Phil's finding the scabbard, which he had picked up in Mr. Smith's stockroom. He told the policeman about it.

Green nodded. "That certainly looks as if the same person who broke into *The Wood Basket* was also interested in the pirate scabbard."

While Freddie had been talking to the policeman, Flossie had been poking around the room. She pushed aside some of the newspapers on the table. As she did so, a snapshot fell to the floor. Flossie picked it up. "Look at this!" she called.

The snapshot showed Freddie and Flossie talking to Casey Browne on the *Jamaica Queen!*

"Why would Shifty Peters have our pictures?" Freddie asked in surprise.

"I don't know," Flossie admitted, "but maybe that's why he looked so scared when he saw us."

"I hope Casey isn't a friend of his," Freddie said worriedly.

By this time the policemen had decided there was no more evidence in the room. They left and walked with the twins back to the hotel.

Mrs. Bobbsey was waiting for them in the lobby. "Where have you been?" she asked. "I looked in all the shops for you."

When Freddie and Flossie told her of their adventure, she smiled. "You *have* been busy! You were very alert to recognize that carving and find the scabbard. I'm proud of you." Freddie and Flossie beamed happily.

The other children were amazed when they heard of the morning's happenings.

Bert frowned. "It sure sounds as though Shifty and Casey are in league. They're both interested in pirates and treasure, remember. Maybe that means something."

"It's very strange." Nan sighed.

"You two had luck finding Shifty this morning," said Phil. "Maybe we'll be lucky enough to locate the hidden treasure when we go to our island this afternoon."

After lunch the six children rode their bicycles down to the dock. They put on life jackets and stepped into the *Hibiscus.*

Jennifer took the tiller while Phil managed the sail. The Bobbseys settled back to enjoy the ride.

"I love sailing on the deep blue sea," Flossie remarked as the breeze ruffled her curls.

The *Hibiscus* skimmed over the water toward Henderson Island in the distance. Several other sailboats were out, and a couple of speedboats darted back and forth across the harbor.

Once on open water Phil and Jennifer relaxed. They and the Bobbseys began to discuss the project of locating the L-shaped cave.

"I thought I'd found about every cave on the island," Phil remarked, "but I haven't noticed any like that."

"We'll have to watch for two tall things, either trees or rocks," Nan reminded him.

Suddenly Freddie sat up straight and pointed across the water. A speedboat was heading right for the *Hibiscus!*

"He's going to hit us!" the little boy shouted.

Jennifer pushed hard on the tiller, trying to change course and avoid the oncoming boat. But she turned too far down wind. The breeze struck the other side of the sail and the boom swung over with a bang.

Jennifer did not have time to duck. The boom struck her a glancing blow and she tumbled into the water as the boat heeled far over.

# CHAPTER XVII

## A CAPTURE

"GIRL overboard!" Freddie shouted when Jennifer was knocked into the water.

Bert stood up, ready to jump in after her.

"She'll be all right," Phil said easily. "Jen's a good swimmer and besides, she has her life jacket on."

By this time, the speedboat was far away. Phil skillfully turned the *Hibiscus* about and with two tacks brought the boat alongside his sister, who was bobbing up and down in the calm sea. Bert and Nan helped her aboard.

"Are you all right?" Nan asked anxiously.

"Sure," replied Jennifer cheerfully. "I often get a ducking when Phil and I are out. My clothes will be dry by the time we reach the island!"

A short while later Phil tied up at the island dock. As the children walked toward the office shack, they stopped in dismay.

*All the tents had been knocked over and lay flat on the ground!*

"How could that have happened?" Nan gasped.

Phil looked grim. "This is the sort of thing that made Father close his sailing school," he said. "Someone's trying to keep people off this island!"

"What a mean trick!" Jennifer declared.

"Well, we can't do anything about it now," Phil said. "We came to find an L-shaped cave. Let's get started!"

"Why don't we divide up for the search?" Bert suggested. "Nan and Freddie could go together; I'll take Jennifer, and you and Flossie can be a pair."

"Okay," Phil agreed. "You all go on. I want to stop in the office to see if everything's all right. Will you wait, Flossie?"

With a nod the little girl sat down on the dock and swung her legs over the side. Phil went into the shack and the other searchers started off.

Bert and Jennifer headed for the far side of the island where they had not looked before. They hunted carefully for signs of caves. The children saw none, but suddenly Bert drew Jennifer back.

"Look!" he whispered. "There's a boat pulled up on that little beach."

"It's the same speedboat that almost ran into us!" the girl declared in a low voice. "I wonder whose it is."

The two children watched for a few minutes, but there was no sign of life around the boat. Finally they walked on.

In the meantime Nan and Freddie were making their way up the other side of the island. They had not gone far when Freddie, who was in the lead, stopped and pointed ahead.

Some distance away was a man. He had his back turned to them and was digging. Nan and Freddie crept closer.

"Shifty Peters!" Freddie whispered excitedly.

"I'll stay here and watch him," Nan proposed. "You run back and see if Phil is still at the shack. He can radio the police."

"Okay!" Freddie slipped away silently and Nan took up her stand behind a tree. The man was still digging.

When Freddie reached the shack he found Bert and Jennifer just telling Phil about seeing the motorboat but nothing else unusual. After hearing Freddie's story, Phil sent off a call to the Kingston police, who said they would send a launch over to the island immediately.

"But Shifty might get away before they come!" Freddie said.

"Bert and I will go back and keep watch with Nan," Phil decided. "Jennifer, you stay here with Freddie and Flossie and wait for the police. Freddie can show them where to come."

Freddie described the spot where Nan was hiding, and the two boys set off. When they reached her, Nan put a finger to her lips. In the distance the boys could see Shifty. He seemed to have finished his digging and was resting under a tree. There was a large burlap bag on the ground beside him.

As the children watched, they were astonished to see a man come from the opposite direction. He stopped to speak to Shifty who jumped up.

"Casey Browne!" Nan cried under her breath. "They *are* working together!"

The pilot appeared to be asking a question. Shifty shook his head violently. The next moment the thief picked up the bag and began to run.

"Hey, wait a minute!" Casey called and raced after him. The men headed toward the hidden children.

"Let's get him, Phil!" Bert urged.

Phil nodded. As the thief ran past their hiding place, the two boys jumped out and tackled him around the knees. Shifty hit the ground with a *thump!* The burlap bag burst open and carved wooden figures scattered over the area.

Shifty hit the ground with a thump.

Bert and Phil sat astride the half-stunned fugitive, pinning him down.

The pilot stared in astonishment at the three children. "Sorry if we've hurt your friend, Casey," Bert said.

"My *friend?*" Casey looked mystified. "I've never seen this man before!"

The pilot explained that he had gone to the Hendersons' home to see the Bobbseys and had been told they were on the island. He had borrowed a boat and come over to find them.

"I ran across this fellow and asked him if he had seen you," Casey continued. "But then he picked up his bag and began to run away!"

"I'm glad you don't know him," Nan spoke up earnestly. "He's a thief!"

Bert looked at Casey. "You never seemed to want to answer our questions," he said. "We couldn't help being suspicious of you!"

Casey put a hand on Bert's shoulder. "You'll just have to trust me," he said quietly. "I'm doing some intelligence work for the government and can't always explain my actions. I *was* in that ruined house outside Port Maria looking for a suspected spy. I dropped the peach stone monkey then."

"That's all right, Casey," Bert replied with a relieved smile. "We won't ask you any more questions."

At this point Shifty tried to free himself. The boys and Casey held on tightly to him.

"The police will be here in a few minutes," Phil told the pilot. "I called them over the short-wave."

While they were waiting, the three children told Casey about the thefts from Mr. Smith's shop and their efforts to solve the mystery.

They had just finished when two policemen arrived with Jennifer and the small twins. "These are Officers Green and Winton," Freddie announced proudly. "Flossie and I met them this morning."

"And a great help you were, too!" Officer Green said with a smile. "And now you've helped to catch Shifty Peters! Incidentally, we found out how he got into *The Wood Basket.*"

In reply to the children's excited questions, the policeman told them that Clark, the locksmith's assistant, had been captured as he was about to fly to Haiti. Clark had broken down and confessed that he had made a duplicate key to Mr. Smith's shop for Shifty Peters.

"How about that, Shifty?" Officer Winton asked the scowling thief.

"Okay," he snarled. "So I took the things!"

"You left a piece of newspaper about Phil in the stockroom," Freddie piped up. "Why?"

Shifty glared at the little boy. "I had a couple

of 'em. Must have dropped one by mistake. I sent the other clipping to a friend of mine who's interested in pirates."

"You must be interested too," Bert declared. "I saw you in the drugstore in Port Maria and the owner said you asked him about Henry Morgan's place. Later you almost ran me down on that country road."

"Who was in the car with you?" Phil asked the prisoner.

"My friend Hansen," Shifty replied.

"Were you also the man in the ruined house who took our car?" Nan asked.

Shifty looked startled, then admitted he had taken the car to discourage the Bobbseys from looking for treasure in that area.

"I had hidden some of my loot in that old house, but when you kids came I decided to dig it up again," he added.

"You buried some under the Cringle Tree, too!" Freddie said accusingly.

"You found that out?" Shifty was amazed. "I never thought anyone would look in such a public place. I buried the stuff in the middle of the night. I'm sure no one saw me."

"A little boy found a wood carving you dropped!" Nan explained.

"You kids have been bad luck for me," Shifty whined. "I was getting desperate for money, so I went into that shop this morning to sell a carving." He pointed to Flossie. "Then this little girl had to recognize it!"

"You stole Phil Henderson's scabbard too, didn't you?" Bert asked. "It was found in your room."

"No. Hansen took it. I was only keeping it for him. He had some crazy idea there was a clue to pirate treasure in the scabbard."

Bert looked at Phil and winked. Neither boy said a word.

"Okay, Shifty," Officer Green said. "What were you doing here on Henderson Island?"

"I was hidin' my things in the entrance to that cave," Shifty replied. "I thought it would be safe. Hansen and I figured we had everyone scared off." He chuckled. "We even played a record of pirate songs and left the kids a warning message!"

Phil had a question. "And I'll bet you damaged my father's boats."

Shifty gave a sullen nod.

"Is that your boat we saw on the other side of the island?" Bert inquired.

Shifty nodded again.

"Was it you who tried to capsize us?" Jennifer asked indignantly.

"I just wanted to keep you from coming to the island," Shifty said defensively.

"Were you alone?" Officer Green queried.

Shifty hesitated, then muttered, "Yes." He also admitted to having knocked over the tents.

Freddie had been thinking hard. Now he spoke up. "Why did you have a picture of Flossie and me with Casey Browne?"

Shifty looked astonished, but replied, "Hansen snapped that on board the *Jamaica Queen*. Later he gave it to me so I could shadow Browne and try to find out if he had located any sunken pirate treasure ships. Hansen wanted Browne to take him up in his plane, but he refused."

"I thought there was something dishonest about that fellow!" Casey exclaimed.

The policeman snapped handcuffs on Shifty. "Come on!" Officer Winton ordered, picking up the bag of stolen articles. "We'll tow your boat."

When they had left, Casey turned to the children. "Just what *are* you kids doing here anyway?"

"Looking for pirate treasure," Bert replied. He told the pilot about their discovery of what they thought was a clue under the word "cave."

"You're pretty good!" Casey said admiringly. "I'd like to help you hunt for that cave."

"We might start with this one," Bert remarked.

They all turned to look at a cave behind them.

The opening was low and almost hidden by a thick growth of bushes and weeds.

Phil surveyed it curiously. "I've found a lot of caves on this island," he said, "but I've never noticed this one."

"Let's go in!" Freddie urged.

The children had flashlights, which they switched on as they crawled into the cave. Casey Browne followed.

Inside, the ceiling was high enough for them to walk erect. They went for some distance in silence, flashing their lights before them. Bert was in the lead. Suddenly he ran ahead.

"The path makes a sharp turn here!" he called back excitedly. "The cave is L-shaped!"

# CHAPTER XVIII

## THE PIRATE TREASURE

AT Bert's cry the other children pressed forward. The cave's path did indeed turn at a right angle!

"Do you suppose this is really the cave J. Morris meant?" Nan cried. Her dark eyes shone with excitement.

"I didn't see any tall trees or rocks near it," Flossie commented.

Her remark made the others stop. They had forgotten the lines on either side of the L in the parchment message!

"Flossie's right! I didn't notice anything like that at the entrance of the cave, did you?" Bert looked at Phil.

The other boy shook his head, then he became more hopeful. "Of course, it's been a long time since J. Morris wrote that note," he pointed out. "Something could have happened to those landmarks."

The children decided that, before investigating the cave further, they should go outside and look for any signs of trees or rocks at the cave entrance. Seeing none, they walked over the ground, carefully searching for clues.

"Here's a big fallen tree," called Nan finally.

"And here's another," Jennifer cried.

The kapok trees lay about five feet away from the cave entrance, one on either side. Both were so overgrown with vines and weeds that they were barely noticeable.

"Do you think these could have been here in J. Morris's time?" Phil asked doubtfully.

Jennifer had an idea. "Don't you remember, Phil, Daddy told us one day about a terrific storm several years ago that blew down many of the big old trees on the island?"

"That's right! These might have fallen over then."

"That's good enough for me!" Bert cried. "Let's go back into the cave and look for the treasure!"

Casey was almost as excited as the children as they made their way along the uneven, rocky floor of the cave. They came to the "L" turn. Then, lights in hand, they proceeded more slowly. Here the ceiling was lower and the sides dripped with moisture.

Nan took Flossie's hand while Jennifer held

Freddie's arm. The two older boys were in the lead. Casey brought up the rear.

"This part of the cave is much deeper," Phil observed. "It must run almost to the shore."

The ceiling was getting lower and lower. By now the older children had to stoop and Casey was practically crawling.

"We're coming to the end!" Bert called out. "We can't go any farther."

"Where's the pirate treasure?" Freddie asked, disappointed.

Bert swung his light in a wide arc. As he did, he caught sight of a dark mass against one side of the passage at the very end of the cave. He crawled up and tapped it with his flash. There was a clink of metal.

"This is it!" Bert cried. "We've found it!"

Everyone scrambled to Bert's side. After further examination by the light of Phil's flash the boys determined that the dark object was a metal chest. It was very heavy.

Casey squeezed past the girls. "I'll help carry it out," he volunteered.

With the girls and Freddie going ahead lighting the way, Casey and the two older boys carried the chest to the cave entrance. There they set it down. They all looked at the metal box curiously. It was blackened with age and dirt.

"Quick!" Freddie cried. "Open it!"

"Put that down!" ordered a harsh voice.

Bert bent over the chest. There was a very rusty lock. "We'll need tools to break it," he said. "Maybe we'd better take the chest to Kingston and work on it there."

Phil stepped forward to help his friend lift the heavy box.

*"Put that down!"* ordered a harsh voice from behind them.

Startled, they whirled around. The twins gasped in recognition. It was Hansen, and he motioned them away with a threatening gesture.

"That chest belongs to me!" he declared with a scowl. "You kids leave it alone!"

Freddie had been standing to one side. Now he slipped quietly behind a bush. When no one noticed, he raced back toward the office shack.

"I'll get the police!" he thought. But when he reached the shack he realized he did not know how to work the short-wave radio.

As the little boy looked around desperately, his eyes fell on the SOS signal flag which lay, neatly folded, on a filing cabinet. Quickly he grabbed it and ran outside. In another second he had fastened it to the rope on the flag pole and pulled it up. The SOS whipped in the breeze!

"I'll wait here for the police," Freddie decided. He stood on the dock, squinting out over the water. "I hope they come before Striped Cap takes the treasure away!"

A few minutes later Freddie was delighted to see the police launch approaching at a fast rate.

"What's up?" called Officer Green, as he got ready to jump onto the dock. "We were on our way back here when we saw your signal."

Quickly Freddie told them about finding the pirate chest and the arrival of Hansen. "He says the treasure is his!" the little boy concluded. "Don't let him take it away."

"We were headed back," Officer Green said grimly, "because Shifty Peters finally admitted Hansen was still on the island."

Back at the cave Hansen approached the metal chest and stooped to pick it up. As he did, Casey stepped back into the cave. Now he signaled Bert and Phil.

Before Hansen realized what was happening, Casey and the boys rushed him. The next minute they had him pinned to the ground.

"You can't do this to me!" Hansen sputtered.

"Shifty Peters gave you away," Bert informed him. "We know you stole the scabbard from Phil's room."

"I had to get it," Hansen muttered. "I was sure it would have some clue to this treasure."

Bert had a sudden thought. "Is that what you were looking for in my cabin on the *Jamaica Queen?*" he asked.

"Yes, and I got caught!" Hansen said in a surly tone. "I overheard you tell Browne you were going to help the Henderson boy solve a pirate mystery, so I thought he must have sent you the scabbard."

Hansen shook his head gloomily. "Everything went wrong! I thought I'd keep you away from Jamaica until I found the treasure so I gave that taxi driver some money to make you miss the ship in St. Thomas."

"But it came back for us!" Flossie interrupted.

Hansen nodded. "I didn't think the captain would do that," he admitted.

"Stand up!" Casey said harshly, jerking the captive to his feet. The pilot backed the man against a small tree and with his belt fastened Hansen's hands behind him around the trunk.

"That will hold you until the police come," Casey remarked.

"I'll radio for them," Phil said quickly. But as he turned, Freddie and the two officers broke through the underbrush.

"Freddie!" Nan exclaimed. "Where have you been?"

"I sent for the police," the little boy explained proudly. "I flew the 'Help' flag!"

"Oh, you're wonderful!" Flossie praised her twin.

The policemen freed Hansen's hands and substituted handcuffs for Casey's belt. While Officer Green herded his prisoner toward the dock, Casey helped Officer Winton carry the chest.

"We'll take this to headquarters and open it when you get there," Winton told the children.

"Anyone want to ride with me?" Casey asked when the police launch had pulled away.

Freddie and Flossie nodded eagerly. They took their places in the speedboat while the older children climbed into the *Hibiscus*. Soon all three crafts were heading toward Kingston.

When the children walked into police headquarters some time later, they found the museum curator, Mr. Masters, waiting with the police chief.

"The chief rang me up to tell me about your find," he explained. "I hurried over to see what is in the chest."

Officer Green brought a hammer and knocked off the ancient lock. Then, while everyone watched breathlessly, Bert and Phil lifted the top.

"Ooh!" Flossie squealed. "The treasure!"

Inside the chest was a jumble of old coins and gold jewelry set with precious stones. Mr. Masters took out a handful of the money.

"Pieces of eight, golden moidores, piasters, doubloons!" he exclaimed in delight as he let the coins drop through his fingers.

The curator turned to the children. "I'm sure the government will be glad to buy this treasure from you for the museum," he said.

The Bobbsey twins and the Hendersons conferred for a few minutes. Then Bert acted as spokesman. "We've had the fun of finding it," he said. "All of us would like to give the treasure to your museum."

Mr. Masters looked overjoyed. "That is very generous," he said. "I shall see that you receive an official acknowledgement and that your names have a prominent place in the museum."

"You can tell the gov'ment that we solved the MYSTERY ON THE DEEP BLUE SEA," said Flossie with a giggle.

"It's a good thing I got Bert for a pen pal," Phil said, beaming.

The children learned from Officer Green that Karen and her family were thrilled at the return of the stolen carvings. The police chief shook hands with each of the young detectives. "You Bobbsey twins have done very well in Jamaica in spite of being such troublemakers," he said with a smile.

"Troublemakers?" Bert echoed in astonishment. "That's one mystery we haven't solved. How did you get that idea?"

The chief told them he had received a letter from a boy in Lakeport telling him that the twins were coming to Jamaica and warning him to be on the lookout as the Bobbseys were always making trouble at home.

"What is the boy's name?" Nan asked indignantly.

The chief picked up a letter from his desk and looked at the signature. "Danny Rugg," he replied.

Bert suddenly grinned. "Wait'll Danny hears we 'troublemakers' found a real pirate treasure!"